TORCHWOOD
First Born

New titles in the Torchwood *series from BBC Books:*

Long Time Dead *by Sarah Pinborough*

First Born *by James Goss*

The Men Who Sold the World *by Guy Adams*

TORCHWOOD
First Born

James Goss

BOOKS

3 5 7 9 10 8 6 4 2

Published in 2011 by BBC Books, an imprint of Ebury Publishing.
A Random House Group Company

Copyright © James Goss 2011

James Goss has asserted his right to be identified as the author of this Work in
accordance with the Copyright, Designs and Patents Act 1988

Torchwood is a BBC Worldwide Production for the BBC and Starz Originals.
Executive producers: Russell T Davies, Julie Gardner and Jane Tranter

Original series created by Russell T Davies,
and developed and produced by BBC Cymru Wales.
BBC, 'Torchwood' and the Torchwood logo are trademarks of
the British Broadcasting Corporation and are used under licence.

The Random House Group Limited Reg. No. 954009

Addresses for companies within the Random House Group can be found at
www.randomhouse.co.uk

A CIP catalogue record for this book is available from the British Library.

ISBN 978 1 849 90283 0

The Random House Group Limited supports the Forest Stewardship
Council® (FSC®), the leading international forest certification
organisation. All our titles that are printed on Greenpeace approved
FSC® certified paper carry the FSC® logo. Our paper procurement
policy can be found at www.randomhouse.co.uk/environment

Editorial director: Albert DePetrillo
Editorial manager: Nicholas Payne
Series editor: Steve Tribe
Cover design: Lee Binding © Woodlands Books Ltd, 2011
Production: Rebecca Jones

Printed and bound in Great Britain by CPI Cox & Wyman, Reading, RG1 8EX

To buy books by your favourite authors and register for offers,
visit www.randomhouse.co.uk

Rhys

'Rhys!'

I opened my eyes. It was the middle of the night. My wife was standing at the end of the bed, alert as a ninja. A heavily pregnant ninja.

'Rhys!' Gwen repeated. Even in the dark, even seven months gone, she was still so pretty. I'm a lucky man.

I sat up. This was important.

'We've got to go,' she said.

My eyes drifted over to the two holdalls by the door. They'd been packed for months. The blue one was for when she went into labour. The black one meant something else.

'Which one?' I asked, peeling off the duvet. It was freezing.

'What?'

'The blue and black bags look the same in the dark,' I explained, reaching for the bedside lamp.

'Don't touch that light!' she hissed.

Ah. So it was the black bag, then. Great. We were about to go on the run, and I was just wearing a pair of boxer shorts.

There was a noise outside. Gwen crossed to the window and peered down at the street. 'They're coming!' she groaned.

I sloughed on a pair of trackie bums and stumbled over to the window. Big solid cars were turning into our road. Big, solid, unmarked cars.

'Who are they?' I asked.

'How should I know?' she groaned. 'There's a queue for us, these days. Come on!'

We ran down the stairs, and into the hall. Gwen stopped and made a face. 'Gotta go pee,' she said.

'Now?' I bellowed in a whisper.

'Junior is using my bladder as a trampoline,' she hissed back at me in frustration. 'Can't help it. Won't be a tic.'

So I stood there, in the draughty hallway, utterly terrified by the sound of my own breathing, aware that the security forces of any number of agencies, countries or secret organisations were right now parking up outside the front door. They had come for us because they wanted us dead, or worse. Scared? I was bricking it.

Not so long ago, my wife worked for a thing called Torchwood. It protected the Earth, sometimes from alien invasions, sometimes from itself. Things had ended pretty badly – the office had got blown up, and the rest of the team were gone. As in dead or left-the-planet gone. The only remaining bit of Torchwood was Gwen Cooper. The last custodian of a lot of alien secrets. My wife.

Who was, just then, complaining about how cold the toilet seat was.

I heard car doors slam outside and people whispering into crackling radios as their shoes crunched along the pavement. Shadows fell across the door, haloed in orange from the street lamps.

'They're here,' I said, tiptoeing back up the stairs.

We'd been prepared. It wasn't just about the

black bag. Oh no. I fumbled with the key ring in my pocket. A tiny bit of technology, no bigger than a coin, probably fell off the back of a flying saucer. I pressed it, and all the car alarms in the street went off. We'd also prepared an escape route out the bathroom window.

We crept through the garden. I kind of regretted that we'd not been there long enough to do much with it – planted a few bulbs, that kind of thing. Bit late for that – I knew we'd never see the place again. We slipped out into the alleyway and got into our getaway car. Nothing flash, just something Gwen had taken from work – a beaten-up minicab – the perfect vehicle for moving through Cardiff at night without getting noticed. Gwen insisted on squeezing her bump in behind the steering wheel. Clearly she'd be in the driving seat. No change there, then.

We set off down the road, and Gwen laughed.

'Goodbye, Cardiff,' she said.

'Who were they?' I asked, as we rolled gently down empty streets. Not too slow, not too fast – not drawing attention.

'No idea,' she said. 'But let's face it, love, we knew they'd come eventually. No one was going to forget about us.'

'Yeah,' I said, glancing at the rear-view mirror. No sign of any pursuit.

'Where are we going?' I asked.

'Oh, no idea,' said Gwen. 'There were plenty of keys in the lock-up. Lots of nice places to choose from. Pick one.'

'OK,' I said. 'Just as long as we'll be safe.'

'Absolutely,' agreed Gwen, flashing me a big smile. 'We're safe now.'

Which was when the helicopter roared overhead.

We both screamed.

'What the hell?' I was still shouting as she threw the car into an abrupt U-turn, and we bombed down a back lane, bumping around wheelie bins.

'We are being chased by a helicopter,' Gwen stated the obvious, as though I'd bloody missed it. There was a tiny edge to her voice. Like it might have been my fault, just a little.

Bullets sparked off the road ahead of us. Warning shots, I hoped.

Gwen just ignored them, throwing us into reverse and then down towards the stadium. Overhanging trees kept the helicopter back a bit as she ploughed on, bouncing up onto the main road and on our way out of the city. We were leaving Cardiff behind us.

The helicopter rose overhead again, spotlights blinded us and more shots were fired, tearing into the tarmac.

'Gwen Cooper! Give yourself up!' a loudspeaker blared.

More shots, and the car swung around again, heading for a pedestrian underpass. Hopefully it would be empty at this time of night.

'Gwen?' I shouted, 'What are you doing? We can't outrun a helicopter in a minicab!'

'Just watch me, love,' she shouted, putting her foot down. And she grinned.

*

Two months later…

'Rhys!'

I opened my eyes. Grey daylight. Thereabouts dawn. My first breath froze in the air in front of me. I looked across at Gwen, sat in a chair cradling our daughter, the two of them wrapped up against the ice like Eskimos.

'Morning, Campers!' I said, trying to be cheery. My feet sank onto the scratchy nylon carpet. The tiny ancient portable television hissed away in the corner. 'Not watching S4C again, were you?' I asked.

'Someone has to,' she groaned, standing up and stretching. 'If it wasn't for us breastfeeding mothers, I swear their audience would be zero.' She yawned, pushing a free hand through her hair. 'I am now an expert on sheep tics. As a result, I am going to take a shower. Look after her, will you?' and she passed me our baby.

Anwen is beautiful. Someone once said that all babies look like Winston Churchill, but that turns out to be a total lie. All babies look like tiny, furious angels.

She's heavier than you'd expect and lumpy in all the wrong places, but I think she's utterly amazing. I tell her this regularly, but she never really gives a sign that she understands. While Gwen stood cursing under the kitten-lick of a shower, I held Anwen, and jostled her and said nonsense to her, which she never seemed to grow tired of. The things you do for the tiniest facial twitch on a baby that may, just may be a gurgle of pure delight. Or regurgitated milk. I also checked to see whether or not she needed changing. I did this very carefully. Anwen can redecorate a room, and I was running out of clean clothes.

For one thing, we didn't have a washing machine. When we went on the run, we started staying in some fairly interesting places. By interesting, I mean utter dumps. The phrase 'Torchwood Safe House' conjures up quite an image, doesn't it? Of a house for starters. But we were currently staying in one of those immobile home caravan things – you know, a giant box on wheels lavishly decorated in Formica and orange. A nasty beige fridge. Any warmth came from a three-bar heater (only one bar working) or, if we fancied a treat, we left the gas hob on. Luxury.

The one advantage of this place was that it was in the middle of nowhere. The caravan park itself was long closed down (there'd been trouble with gypsies or something – plus who would stay here?) and the nearby village was a stubbornly un-picturesque bit of North Wales. We'd been here a few days and no one had paid us any attention, which was a good sign. At least it looked as though we'd be able to stay here for a while before They found us. Lord alone knows who 'They' were, but we kept moving on, like the Littlest Hobo, only with better rows. Since giving birth to Anwen (no, we don't talk about the actual birth, thank you very much – the head-spinning scene of *The Exorcist* but at the wrong end), Gwen had become even more paranoid – although in her more rational moments, she'd announce that eventually They would stop looking for Us. She'd say it dandling Anwen on her knee which was kind of weird – 'Soon They'll stop trying to kill Mummy and Daddy, won't that be lovely? Oh yes it will!' But to be fair, it was all fairly horrible – the shitty houses, the imminent death by Men In Black... but most of all, having a baby was a bloody nightmare.

We were so tired we'd gone beyond cross-tired and well into exhausted. The killer thing is breastfeeding, since you ask. Now, unlike childbirth itself, breastfeeding is agony for both parents – it's quite something when you're delighted to have had three solid hours of sleep. It's like Anwen is some creepy alien creature that has somehow enslaved us to a life of constant misery. We get no praise (beyond the occasional smile that's mostly trapped wind), just a lot of screaming if we do anything wrong or have failed to anticipate her needs instantly and correctly. And we love her for it. You hear people banging on about suspected terrorists placed under control orders – unable to leave the house, have any free time, and subject to a strict curfew. This is viewed to be cruel and inhumane. Forget it – it's the story of my life. Only give a few of these suspect terrorist buggers a newborn baby, and they'd crack within seventy-two hours.

I know what you're thinking. 'That's all very well, but neither you nor Gwen have a job.' Yeah. Right now I'd love to have a job, to be able to get out of here for just a few hours a day. Just for a break. Right now Rhys Williams would kill to hear about purchase orders or invoices or spreadsheets. Hell, I'd even sit through a sales meeting with Evil Josephine From Newport (a lass who has mastered the art of being simultaneously boring and creepy). *Anything* other than sit around Baby-this and Baby-that-ing with Gwen.

No, since you ask. Not a great time. I think we still loved each other. But it was hard to tell. I'd have loved us to get pissed and have a laugh, but we couldn't ('Because of the milk,' said Gwen), so we just didn't. 'Have a beer, go on,' she'd say. I'd sit, drinking it with the solid grimness of an old man while Anwen stared at me. 'That's Daddy. He's having his happy juice,' Gwen would say. Great.

I finished the near-radioactive job of changing the nappy as Gwen emerged from the shower. She was wearing a towel burqa, it was that cold. All I could see were her eyes gazing critically at my nappy changing. You'd think I'd never wiped an arse before. But I said nothing, applied a fresh nappy and then realised.

'Balls. That's the lot. No more nappies.'

'Oh,' said Gwen. She leaned back against the door.

'I think there's a bag in the car,' I said. 'But maybe I should pop into town to get some.'

'Town?' her tone was guarded.

'The village. Rawbone.'

'Right. It's not a town. We'll be lucky if it's got a shop.'

'It might have. Failing that, I saw a superstore a few miles back. I can drive there.'

Gwen shook her head. 'CCTV. Best not.'

'OK.' This was one of Gwen's Mad Policies. Avoid getting on CCTV. Which sounds sensible. Fine, let's avoid the big supermarkets. But every time we fill up with petrol we're on camera. ATMs are out – not that there's anything much in our accounts, probably. We're managing with a car boot of cash that Gwen got from the storage unit.

'Village shop it is, then.' I cracked a smile at her. 'Hey, what about it? Fancy a walk into the village?'

Gwen looked tempted and hopeful for a moment. Then Anwen made a noise. A tiny, intuitive little noise that could have been a cry, could have been a hiccup. No Freedom For You, Mother. Gwen shrugged, helplessly. 'Perhaps not today, eh?' she said. Her smile wasn't even 40 watt. She picked up Anwen's leaden weight and flopped into a chair covered in bobbly green nylon felt. 'Go on,' she sighed, 'go have fun,' like she was giving me a pass to Tiger Tiger.

I grabbed the keys from the lock, trying not to look at the fob that said 'I. Jones', and stepped out into the crisp, crisp air. It was one of those doors that there's a knack to closing. You know, handle up, handle down, spin round three times, slam.

I set off, then risked a backward glance. Gwen was feeding Anwen, but the baby looked up at me, and fixed me with a stare. I made a little bye-bye wave and trudged off down the hill. I was wearing my pyjamas. But I didn't care. It was raining only slightly. Great.

As I trudged towards the first house, I reached a sign announcing this was Rawbone to anyone who cared. I noticed a patch of flowers growing around the sign and into the hedgerow. They were odd, like giant, rotten tulips. Bloody funny things, I thought, and wondered why no one had got around to pulling them up. They reeked.

The village was tiny. I guessed that if I met anyone I'd give them my best 'hello' nod. You know, the nod that city-folk use when they're in the country that says 'I mean you no harm and do not fear your easy familiarity. Please go about your business, noble rustic.'

But there was no one. There was a village

shop – it was one of those good old-fashioned front rooms. Where you'd normally have a sofa there was a lot of tins, and there was a chiller cabinet where you'd expect to find the telly. The shop was almost empty – a dark-haired teenage girl stood serving a middle-aged woman with lots of grey hair and a grey cardigan.

'Will that be all, Miss Eloise?' the girl asked, almost impossibly politely.

'Yeah, that'll do nicely, Jenny,' said the woman with a surprising American drawl. She shuffled past me, grunted a brief 'Hey there!' and was gone.

The girl Jenny looked at me. 'You are new,' she announced. 'I will go and get Mother.' She ducked through an orange ribbon curtain before I even had a chance to ask where the nappies were.

I was alone in the shop. There was no one behind the counter. So I stood there, humphing and harring, and then started to hunt down baby stuff. Another example of how beloved Anwen had rewritten my brain – previously my tiny head would automatically scope out the fire exits and all the ingredients for spag bol. Now it just looked for nappies and wipes.

Only there weren't any. Puzzler.

'Morning!'

The shopkeeper was a smiling woman in her early forties. She was plainly dressed – like she'd settled for floral print a few years early. She was wearing a pinny and had clearly come from the back of the house – beyond the cash register was the distant warmth of a kitchen and a burbling radio.

'Hello,' I said awkwardly. I felt like I was intruding in her home.

'Can I help you?' she prompted gently.

'Yes,' I said. 'I'm looking for nappies. Bit of a crisis.'

'No,' she said after a long pause. Which was odd. But the way she said the word was even odder. Very firm.

'Not to worry,' I said. 'You know what babies are like.'

'Not really,' she replied, her fingernails digging away at the oil cloth covering the counter.

'Ah,' I said. 'We're staying at the caravan park. Mobile home a friend gave us the keys to. For a bit.'

'I see.' Her tone was disapproving.

I decided to win her over. After all, she had the monopoly on crisps and chocolate for five miles. I turned on the full charm, learned her name (Mrs Meredith) and tried ever so hard to make the old dear smile. But smile came there none. Her lips just got tighter and tighter as my small talk petered out. An awkward silence settled between us, and my gaze drifted down to the foam bananas. Inspiration struck. 'Got any papers?'

Mrs Meredith dug under the counter and dropped a pile of newspapers on the counter with an impressive thump. Ah, news – lovely. With no internet and half a digital telly channel, we were finding it hard keeping up with current events. It'd been a while since I'd seen a paper. I picked through them.

'Oh, "Lady Gaga link to Cancer"?'

Mrs Meredith tutted. 'Yes I know. Shocking isn't it?'

'Bloody unbelievable,' I said, a bit too crossly.

We looked at each other. I was sharply reminded of the time when a hairdresser asked me if I had any pets. 'No, no,' I'd told him. 'If I did, it'd probably be a dog. And just the one, though. You don't want to be one of those mad people with three cats now, do you?'

To which, inevitably, the hairdresser had replied, 'I have three cats myself, actually,' and got on with cutting my hair.

It was a similar, awkward feeling.

I bought a copy of the paper anyway, and grabbed a Mars bar as well. Walking back up the hill, I suddenly realised how wrong this was. I should have got two. But I hadn't. And if I had, Gwen would have said how whey protein or e-numbers or whatever would get into her milk and Kill The Baby. But I couldn't just walk back in with one bar. It would look selfish, and I didn't much fancy going back to the shop.

So I ate the chocolate bar in the rain as I walked home. I took a little wander round the village. Scoping out my territory. A crummy pub with a peeling plastic sign advertising sport, some houses that seemed to be fifty years old, a church. Someone whizzed past me on a bike – dark hair, wrapped up against the weather, Celtic-looking. Teenager. A bit of life. I nodded, but he didn't nod back, just cycled down the road and away. Oh-kaaaayy.

I walked on a little further. No rain, really. Another kid went past on another bike. Or was it the same kid, same bike? I tried saying hello, but again no answer. Just a dark-haired boy pedalling off down the street.

A battered jeep rattled past, driven erratically by the scatty-looking lady I'd seen in the village shop. As she drove past, she stared at me. As though it was odd seeing a stranger around. Welcome to your new home, I thought.

I went back up the hill, vaguely aware that someone was watching me. But no one I could see. Perhaps it was the kid on the bike. But I couldn't see him. Just a vague sense of unease, of being followed.

I passed those strange flowers again, and paused, trying to work out what their smell was. Farty dog and boiled cabbage – mixed with a strange muskiness that reminded me of the BO of a lorry driver I used to work with. A smell that you could chew.

I walked through the caravan graveyard and wrestled open the door, trying to climb in before I let out all the heat. Gwen nodded to me as she woke up from a nap. 'No nappies,' I explained. 'Looks like we're due a trip out. This place is weird.'

Gwen

I dreamed that it was raining burning cars.

One by one they fell from the night sky, almost drifting before they bounced a bit on the tarmac.

Walking between them with surprising grace was a handsome man in an old military uniform. He looked like a freshly retired model, only he was carrying a very large gun and shooting casually up into the sky. His name was Captain Jack Harkness.

I couldn't quite see where the burning cars were coming from, but they were raining down thick and fast.

'Over there,' said a voice beside me. I turned. A young man, impossibly neat and dapper, stood next to me, straightening his already symmetrical tie. This was Ianto Jones. It was a hot summer's night but he was wearing a three-piece suit and holding a rocket launcher like it was a furled-up umbrella.

Jack, Ianto, Gwen. We were Torchwood. We were saving the world. Right now.

I looked behind me to where something very large, angry and made of flame was throwing the cars off the motorway bridge. As far as I could tell, the vehicles were abandoned. I hoped they were. Most of them landed near us but I watched as a flaming Saab fell short and vanished into the river with a pfssht *as it extinguished.*

Jack dodged a melting people-carrier and

sauntered up to us. 'Gwen Cooper!' he boomed. 'Glad you made it. Did you remember the bomb?'

'Of course she remembered the bomb,' muttered Ianto. 'Gwen never forgets.'

'Silly me.' Jack smiled like we were having fun. Which, oddly, I guess we were. 'Right then, let's go to work.'

I woke up as Rhys came in, letting all the warmth out while he cludged around taking his shoes off and grunting at me. He had chocolate round his chops – bet he thought that was the perfect crime. Oh, I'd kill for some chocolate. Or a nice bit of cake. Christmas cake with rum and marzipan. Bet I'm not allowed *any* of the ingredients of that. Or maybe they've changed their minds over the weekend – like they do. For all I know, it's probably compulsory to eat blue cheese and raw shellfish by the scoopful. I stared glumly at the paper he'd plonked down on the counter. It was just bound to contain yet more things which will INSTANTLY KILL YOUR BABY.

I'd rather not risk it, thanks.

So it looked like Rhys and I would be off to the supermarket. That much I knew. I could have let him go on his own, but I didn't dare. He'd probably have come back with a bag of chips and some magic beans.

We clambered into the car and drove away. Well, I say that. We fitted the child seat, stuffed the back full of nappies, wipes, bin bags, a change of clothes for Anwen and a couple of spare sweaters in case one of us got a hasty respray, blankets, rugs, her favourite little plastic thing... all of it fetched from the caravan. Rhys thinks I should store it all in the car, but I never quite get round to sorting it out, and I keep telling him 'Ah, it won't take a minute.' To think we used to just dive into cars and roar off, outrunning Scary Men In Black Cars. These days we couldn't even escape a milk float without a fortnight's notice.

We drove away from Rawbone, and I had an urge to say 'Let's not go back.' There'd be a reason why we had keys to that desolate caravan. There was always a reason why Torchwood had keys. Sometimes it was to store files or things best forgotten. Sometimes it was unfinished business. Rawbone had an air about it of unfinished business. It looked so forlorn.

Three weeks later...

Rhys had planted potatoes. It was like he'd settled. I was even letting him off the leash – you know, going down the pub for an evening pint. It spared me from having him hang around the caravan all the time like a pining dog. Of course, bless him, he was so knackered, two pints and he would be plastered.

He'd made friends, though. That was nice. Although I hoped I would never meet any of them. I love Rhys dearly, but it's like he gets his mates from a pound shop. His new friends would all be from North Wales, so god knew what they'd be called – they name their kids anything around here – Bluebell, Lorry, Tesco Clubcard.

The great thing was it gave him a little bit of freedom and me the chance to sneak a cheeky nap. Which was nice.

It was too good to last. He had an airy, casual look to him as he put the bottles in the steriliser. 'Hey, hey!

How are the two women in my life?' he asked.

'One is asleep, the other is dead on her feet,' I said.

'What you girls need is a break. A change of scenery.' A pause. A spontaneous grin. Here it bloody comes. 'I know! Let's go down the pub.'

I waved this away quickly. 'No, no, you go. Go on.'

But Rhys stood his ground. 'It's like you're in prison here. Come on, love, we can do this. How long is it since you've been out on a proper trip?'

I tried to answer. 'Lots, I've been out loads!'

'Not counting shopping or nipping to the garage.'

'Oh,' I mumbled.

'Or wheeling her around the caravan park in the pram.'

'Damn.' I laughed.

Rhys smiled, triumphant. 'It will be Fun. And if it isn't, I promise you can never let me hear the last of it.'

'Can I make your life hell?' I grinned.

He nodded. 'Get your coat, pet.'

Of course, Rhys hadn't quite got the new baby thing – he was still impatiently bouncing Tigger Rhys, assuming that it takes me longer to get ready than him because... well, it's what women do. But it's not like that. Not with Anwen. Everything just takes so much time.

'I'll give her a change,' he offered like it was an offer to dance on hot coals.

'Yeah, yeah.' I waved him away. 'But I'm going to feed her before we go out. I am not popping out a boob in public. Not ready for that yet.'

I caught Rhys's expression. 'Do not say anything.

Especially not about getting turned on.'

'Would not dream of it,' he vowed with a smirk.

We made it out of the caravan in just under forty minutes (which was good going) and rolled the pram down into the village. I wrinkled my nose at a sudden stench. 'Is that Anwen?'

Rhys grinned. 'Nah, it's the stink thistles. That's what they call them.' He pointed to a patch of green by the roadside. 'They're all around the village. God alone knows what they'll smell like in summer.'

'Do they have summer here?'

'Probably not.'

We pottered down the road towards the solitary street lamp. 'So what's the occasion?' I asked Rhys.

He smiled. 'A welcome party. For us. It's a surprise.'

Surprise Party. Those two words fill me with alarm almost as much as Alien Invasion.

As soon as I saw the pub, I knew what it was going to be like. It was one of those places – you think that a country pub should be an ancient building, possibly thatched with a sign swinging gently in the breeze. But this was a single-storey, red-brick rectangle with a name picked out in gold letters ('Y Gwyr'), and a satellite dish stapled to the flat roof. Someone had long ago decided, 'Fine, this'll do.'

Well, it was an OK pub, actually. Not exactly 'Ooh, there be strangers in these parts,' but not in any danger of being mistaken for a wine bar, either. It was a box of people and booze. The benches were buttoned-green pleather that had been chewed over by a fair few dogs, the floor was covered in that weird crunchy black carpet you only see in pubs. The odd tuft of tinsel was still sellotaped to the artex ceiling. Billboards were covered with creased adverts with tear-off phone numbers. Music played. I say music – a kind of easy-listening cock rock. The Eagles doing a salute to an album of panpipes covers.

The thing that struck me as we walked in was the sound of real spoken Welsh. North Wales, the land where Welsh is a living language and not a plaything for making personal calls at work and getting great customer service off British Gas. You can be as fluent as you like in Welsh, but if you come from Cardiff, the first time you hit North Wales it's quite a shock. It's not exactly a different language, but I guess it'd be like an Ancient Roman turning up in modern Italy and discovering that Latin's had the builders in.

I tried earwigging, but caught only the odd word and then realised it was petering out, gently fading into English as people noticed me and Rhys. I heard *baban* a few times, though. That was one word I knew. I wondered... was it Anwen they were talking about?

Rhys settled us around a table sticky with spilt beer. Sat across from us were two men called Josh and Tom who were grinning nervously in that 'hello, I am going to try and make friends with you' way that people do.

Interesting.

What the hell were these two doing in the middle of Nowhere, North Wales? Tom was tiny, with red hair that went everywhere and Josh was so poised even his teeth looked ironed. He was also...

'Indian,' said Josh, catching my look, which made me feel bad. 'They were advertising for some diversity, and they got a gay Indian.'

'Who was born in New Zealand,' put in Tom happily.

'Right,' I said. 'But what made you come here?'

'Oh...' Josh squeezed Tom's shoulder. 'We met on a night out in Swansea. I said, "Take me to paradise," and he brought me here...' Josh sighed. 'I would have settled for one grubby night of passion in a Travelodge. But sadly it wasn't to be.'

'I work here,' admitted Tom awkwardly.

'I raise our cat and do some really disastrous things to ladies' hair in the nearest town. Not for money. It's just a hobby.' Josh leant over and poked Rhys in the gut. 'Get us some drinks, big fella.'

'Oh, right.' Rhys started to slouch to the bar.

'And yes, we will be talking about you,' Tom called after him.

Rhys steered almost unconsciously towards a young woman wearing a leopard-print micro-skirt and a denim jacket. She was looking up at the old television, and carefully not paying any attention to Rhys. God love you, girl, I thought, you're so bloody obvious. Luckily, I'd trained Rhys well and he barely cast her a glance.

Josh played with Anwen, while Tom kept an impressive amount of distance. He looked at me apologetically. 'Sorry, Gwen, I'm just terrified I'd break her. It is a her, yeah?'

'Yes,' I said. 'Would you like to hold her?'

Tom shook his head hurriedly.

Josh glanced up from hypnotising Anwen with his fingers. 'Don't take offence, Gwen. Tom's clumsy. He can't make toast without breaking eggs.'

Tom said, 'That's not true. I mowed the lawn.'

'And won't stop going on about it.' Josh held up Anwen and stared into her eyes. 'So, Rhys says your mummy was a policewoman.'

Did he, now? 'Yeah. But I have given up my life of fighting crime. For the moment. You know...'

Tom fished out a phone and started fiddling with it. He caught my glance. 'Oh, no reception for me either. Bloody rubbish, isn't it? I've got used to that, but I refuse to give up Angry Birds.' He was soon immersed in it while Josh and I played with Anwen.

We talked on. Rhys brought over the drinks. I sipped at a lime and soda. Rhys drank his pint like he was an 8-year-old chugging juice. Despite myself, I was having trouble staying awake. Yawn after yawn crept out from behind my hands, but I made a game effort to look as wide awake as possible. Tonight was kind of fun, really, but I was just so tired and the room was so dark.

People came and stopped by the table. I felt a bit like I was being paid court to. But it was mostly Anwen. There was Mrs Harries, a nice lady of a certain age who ran a small school ('But we won't be seeing you for a good few years, will we, young lady?' she said to Anwen, which just about summed Mrs Harries up). A young couple drifted in – the kind of people that reminded me of folks from the Valleys come to Cardiff for a nose round the shopping centre – tall Davydd in sports gear and wet-look hair gel who stared at the ground, and a girl called Sasha who claimed to be a victim of Josh's hair stylings. She didn't stop at the table long, and seemed a bit nervous, as though she was intruding, or scared of me.

Sasha went over to the bar, but as far away as she could from the girl in the leopard print. Interesting. She looked like she was dressed for the Battle of St Mary Street (fought in Cardiff city centre, every weekend). Yet she was sat here on her own, laughing very loudly at whatever was said to her. She glanced in my direction once, and smiled. It was a warning smile. You know the kind I mean – Keep Your Distance, Thanks.

'Odd,' I remarked.

'Nah,' muttered Tom, snicking open a pack of crisps. 'That's just Nerys. She's getting oiled before catching the bus to the Tango.'

'What's the Tango?'

'Winner of the Worst Club In North Wales since 2007,' groaned Josh. 'Full of puking teenagers, farmers having a mid-life crisis and Nerys. She's been a fixture longer than the pole-dancing pole.'

'Do not ask.' Tom helped himself to a handful of crisps and returned to Angry Birds.

I turned to Rhys, who was on his second pint and as genial as the Buddha. 'This is where you spend your evenings?'

He shrugged. 'Beats the caravan.'

'Everything beats the caravan.'

I heard a ker-click and a flicker at the corner of my retina. 'Did someone just take a picture of us?' I asked. The table shrugged. I was worried – who and why? Had Rhys and I been recognised?

'You're celebrities,' grinned Tom, opening a fresh packet of crisps (where did he put it all?).

'Really?'

'Nothing ever happens here,' Josh sighed. 'Imagine how they reacted when I first turned up!' He pointed to the deep tan of his face. 'First time they'd ever seen wheelie luggage.'

I had to go to the bathroom to feed Anwen. It was the last thing I felt like doing in a roomful of strangers. I set up my stall – it's a long and complicated business, made worse by the clothes. If men had to breastfeed there'd be something practical and shaping with lots of useful zips. As it is, you end up spending endless daydreaming hours cooking up a fetching dungaree-blouse-cardigan number. I unbuckled and plugged Anwen in, catching a glimpse of myself in the mirror. I looked tired. And so fat. Like a whale. Like a whale in jeans with an elasticated waist. They were the highlight of my pregnancy and I wasn't giving them up. Not until I'd miraculously shed all the extra pounds. I kept on telling myself it was just milk, but I suspected my sudden addiction to oven chips in the last few months of pregnancy was something to do with it.

'You don't mind having a fat mummy, do you?' I asked Anwen, but she just glared back at me, mildly annoyed that I was talking to her while she fed. Anwen took after her dad – she did a great frown at the tiniest interruption when she was eating.

I kept thinking that I'd be able to go jogging, or down the gym or... I dunno. Eat something fresh. Part of Anwen's Loving Tyranny meant that our baby was looked after in luxury and care while her servants ate out of tins. I was desperate for a spot of freedom or a fresh vegetable. Not on the horizon in the near future.

The bathroom itself was one of those chilly pub toilets that was bolted on as a breeze-block afterthought. A cistern dripped and clicked annoyingly. Anwen opened her eyes and frowned at it.

The door opened, and Sasha came in. I met her eyes. 'Hiya!' I said.

She'd frozen. Well, come on, luv, it's just a bit of boob, surely it's not a trauma.

'Oh,' she said.

'Yeah?' I sounded ruder than I meant to. I felt a bit self-conscious – this thin young woman staring boggle-eyed at my breast. Not even hiding it, just gawping. 'What's up?' I asked her. I could feel myself start to flush with embarrassment, but then thought, *No, stand your ground.*

Sasha nodded absently, but continued to gawp. Something wasn't right.

Then I realised. It wasn't me she was looking at. She was staring at Anwen, riveted. 'What's her name?' she asked haltingly.

I told her, and she repeated Anwen's name a couple of times. Then she leaned forward. 'She's so tiny,' she said.

I agreed with her. Thing you learn about being a mother – people say a lot of dumb stuff to you. My little darling has been called everything. I've heard her referred to as 'quite the little madam', or just-like-her-dad (because that's Rhys, under a foot long and hairless). So Sasha cooing over my baby seemed somehow a bit more normal.

Only she didn't then go and have a pee, or tidy her make-up or anything. She just kept staring at Anwen, talking to her, which since Anwen was still clamped to my breast was a bit... I mean, odd. I disengaged madam gently, and fastened myself up, trying not to make a thing of it. Momentarily thwarted from her all-u-can-eat milk buffet, Anwen hiccupped out a couple of cries, her frowning face threatening worse to come. I was having none of it, and swiftly eyeballed her, but Sasha was genuinely upset.

'Is she all right? She seems so sad, so sad...' And a hand reached out to try and comfort my daughter.

No, I thought. There was just something about Sasha. Wrong. A feeling I got off her. Instinctively, I pulled Anwen back, and Sasha's hand froze.

'I just wanted to touch her,' she implored. Madly, tears formed in her eyes. 'Can I touch her? Please?'

It was an awkward moment – both of us kind of poised, the baby in between us like we were King Solomon's Wives. More than anything, *anything*, I wasn't going to let her touch my baby. I broke away, gathering up my little stall as Sasha started to babble.

'She looks so lovely.' She was wistful. 'And she smells so wonderful.'

'Yeah, milk and vomit,' I said lightly, but just wanting to get out of there.

Sasha stared at me. 'Oh no! She smells just lovely.'

I nodded to her, ignored the plaintive tone in her voice, and went back out to the lounge. Weird.

A bloke at the bar said, 'Let me get you a drink.'

That hasn't happened to me for ages – sometimes, when I was a copper, I'd get strange men offering to buy me drinks at bars all the time. Likely boys. You know how it is.

This guy was young. He looked familiar – oh, of

course, Sasha's boyfriend, wasn't he? He was looking at me with puppy-dog eyes. Mid-twenties, stubbly sideburns, thin as a rake, tracksuit hanging off him like he was made of coat hangers. He was smiling at me. I noticed everyone else was still looking at me a bit warily – Strangers In Town. So I gave him a smile back. Warm and welcoming.

'Davydd, isn't it?'

'Yeah.' His breath was a bit beery and he was grinning widely. 'What would you like? Must be great to go out on the lash again,' he said.

'Just a lime and soda,' I said to him, firmly. 'Still breastfeeding, so I can't really drink. Not without a stopwatch and a calculator. No idea when that'll end. Can't wait to get pissed.'

The barmaid handed me the drink. As she did so, she said, 'Well, I hope you're not using the bottle yet, are you?' And then she stared at me. Clearly expecting a response.

I found this frankly unwelcome. Maybe I should have been used to it, but I wasn't. Oh, lordy. The thing I'd never expected about pregnancy and motherhood was that utter strangers would offer you advice. Including their own infallible solution to the Da Vinci Code that is breastfeeding.

'Er...' I began.

Then someone else butted in. 'No offence, but she looks a little overweight, if you don't mind me saying.'

The barmaid nodded. 'They do say that can happen.' She flashed me a sympathetic look. 'But I've heard it soon shifts when they move onto solids... She's not on solids yet, is she?'

'I, ah...'

An old guy looked up from his pint. 'Mind you don't let her sleep on her side, that's all I'm saying.'

'What?' If I sounded angry, no one noticed.

'Oh no, Ifor, it's sleeping on the front you've got to be careful of. Pay no attention to him, my dear.'

And on it went. Madness. Finally sensing my discomfort, Davydd firmly picked up our drinks and gestured towards the distant table. We glided through the bar, and I flushed slightly at the attention we were getting.

'What the hell was that?' I hissed at him. 'I take it you don't get many strangers here, then?'

He shook his head, puppyish again. 'No, no, not many visitors,' he said. 'And none with babies. Not for a long time You're very special, Gwen.'

'Really?' I was surprised. The one thing you can practically guarantee about North Wales is that every bus is chocka with young mums on missions.

'Not so many babies here, no,' said Davydd. He looked at me oddly.

So that was our first evening out in Rawbone. A few friends. A couple of odd close encounters. A slight air of mystery. Nothing dangerous. But a lot that should have told me something was wrong. If I hadn't been so damn tired.

A few days later, I nipped into the village shop all by myself. It was a bright day and I just had to grab some coffee. That was the excuse, but I felt like a bit of fresh air and proving my independence – hush now, sauntering a quarter of a mile down the road and back felt like a major achievement. The street was empty, so I left Anwen parked up outside in her pram and dashed in. The woman behind the counter beamed at me.

'Good morning, Mrs Meredith,' I said politely.

'We've got nappies now!' she bellowed excitedly.

'Right,' I said.

'Do you want to see the nappies?' she urged, like she had a missing reel of the Zapbruder footage.

'Oh, it's OK,' I replied. 'I'm just after some coffee, really.'

The woman's face fell. 'We got them in specially for you.'

I bought a jar of instant and some nappies. She also pressed a newspaper on me.

'Says here there's an increased risk of cervical cancer if you drink caffeine while you're breastfeeding. You're not planning on doing that, are you, my love?'

I was tempted to ask her for a can of Red Bull.

When I left the shop, Sasha was standing, crouched over the pram, holding Anwen. It's that whole and-this-is-why-you-should-never-leave-your-baby moment. Startled, she flushed with guilt, but she didn't say anything. I couldn't say anything. There weren't words. We just stood, looking at each other.

Sasha held Anwen to her, then steadily uncurled her.

'She was crying,' she said simply, tears pouring down her hot cheeks as she babbled away. 'I was just passing, I just wanted to make sure she was all right...' She rested her down in the pram, tucking the blanket around her.

Still speechless, I stared at Sasha. I reached forward, retucking the blanket. There was nothing wrong with the way that Sasha had done it, but I had to do it again for myself. I could sense the blood warming my face. I was just so angry and scared. I grabbed the pram and wheeled it around, striding back home.

Sasha didn't say anything, just watched me go.

I walked back up the hill, still furious with myself. A kid cycled past me – whose was it? A dark-haired teenager. All the kids in this village had lovely dark hair, the love children of The Beatles. Celtic pride. I guess it was a North Wales thing. All the children looked racehorse-handsome – or at least, they would do when they were a bit older. Another bicycle whizzed past – at first I thought it was the same kid, but then I realised it was a different colour of bike. Same hair, same school uniform. Rhys had come back from a walk one day and announced that all the kids here looked like brothers. I guess that's what happens in a small village. As I passed the stink thistles, a couple more bikes followed me up the hill at a distance. Like crows.

I didn't care. I just wanted to get Anwen and me back inside and shut out the world.

A couple of hours later, there was a knock at the caravan door. It took me a while to answer it – it's cumbersome getting up and going anywhere these days. The knock was repeated.

Davydd was stood outside, shifting from left foot to right foot, from right foot to left foot. He looked stricken. I didn't want this. I really didn't want this. Not now. Actually, not ever.

'Yeah?' I said.

'It's about Sasha,' he said, hideously awkward.

'I guessed,' I said. Truth to tell, the last thing I wanted a chat about. I was furious with her, but also cross with myself. I told myself that nice, normal, properly slept Gwen Cooper would have handled it better.

'Can I come in?' His tone was definitely 'Can I stroke the kitten?'

I pushed the door a bit wider. 'Sure, come on in. Rhys will be back any minute.'

He stepped in, stamping his feet, shaking off his shoes and generally hovering. He looked guilty and nervous. In my police days he would have been a dead ringer for the chief suspect's best friend who'd turn up at the station to say 'What it is, see, is…'

I put the kettle on to boil. This involved sticking one of those camping kettles on the feeble gas hob and waiting for it to defy the laws of physics and shriek like a hen-night. Of course, if you let it get that far it would invariably wake Anwen up, and I wanted her asleep for this. Between the two of us, we'd managed almost an entire hour without a feed or a murmur. How I longed for the day when I'd be able to plonk her in front of CBeebies while I had a nap. I tiptoed over the cold lino and reached down a couple of mugs and ferreted around for the coffee. So, too much caffeine was bad when breastfeeding, was it? Great. Thanks. How was I supposed to cope for a fortnight until someone said that actually not enough caffeine was bad for breastfeeding? I damned them all, spooned three heaps of instant into my mug and turned to confront Davydd. He really was just a chinless boy with a big nose and a whiff of cheap deodorant, nervously fingering the gold chain around his neck. There was the tiniest fuzz of chest hair poking through the top of his white running top. Bless.

'So,' I breezed. Say hello, boys and girls, to Gwen Cooper's best Witness Interview Smile.

'Yeah...' He nodded, cupping his mug like a teddy bear and tracing his fingers over and over the rustic wheatsheaf pattern. 'Look, Gwen, I'm really sorry about Sasha. She's in bits about what happened.'

'What did happen, exactly?' I said, carefully, trying to win him over to my side. 'Cos, I'm not being funny, but she came across as... well, you just can't go around holding other people's kids.'

'I know,' sighed Davydd. 'Listen, what it is, see...' *Bingo.* 'It's... Well, she can't have kids.' He spread his arms out.

'Right,' I said. Instant sympathy. I mean, that was awful.

'We tried.' His voice was a flat whisper, all the pain ironed out of it. 'We tried so hard. Everything. She even got pregnant a couple of times, but it didn't... carry through, if you know what I mean.' His hands gripped the mug real tight.

'I'm sorry,' I said without thinking. 'It must have been—'

'It was bloody horrible,' he groaned, shaking his head. 'Bloody horrible. She got so excited, both times, but I just knew... I knew it was no good. But I couldn't say.' His milk-pale face looked up at me, the bags under his eyes red. He looked so young. So young for all this. 'There are some things you just can't talk about, can you?'

'No,' I said, quietly.

'So, anyway... you know... we've... well, we've taken a kid in now. And she's happy. Sasha is happy.

She loves Brian. Really she does. Next best thing. Lovely bright lad.' Davydd's fingers ran through his close-cropped, gelled hair. He was nervous. 'But... but it's not the same, is it? I mean, fine by me... but not by Sasha. You know. No other young mums in the village, so she's not going to be reminded of it. But then you turn up... Well, she can't help but see how perfect your little one is.' He smiled, a lovely, radiant little smile. 'She's gorgeous, isn't she?'

'Yes,' I agreed. Anwen stirred and gurgled quietly in her sleep. I stroked her softly and wondered what she was dreaming about.

'You're so lucky,' sighed Davydd, looking at the baby and then at me. 'You've got it all. Sasha's just... She can't be like you.' His face lit up with street-preacher zeal. 'Oh! It's so wonderful what you're doing.'

'No, no, it's not, it's rubbish,' I assured him, pushing the hair from my face. 'I am beyond tired, I'm sore in all the wrong places, and my brain is mush. But it's just what I have to do for my daughter. I would do anything for her.'

Davydd's smile widened. 'You're very special,' he said, putting his mug down. 'Oh Gwen, I think you're so special.'

Then he kissed me.

Rhys

So, got back from the garage to find my wife snogging another bloke.

It was the sound of pasties hitting the floor that alerted them. Gwen's eyes were already 200 per cent wide when I walked in, but they stretched that little bit further. The bloke, that scrawny Davydd runt from the village, was up and leaping about like a startled whippet.

'Rhys!' cried Gwen.

'Later!' I snapped, and landed one on Davydd. He dropped back across the sofa. Result. 'Actually,' I breathed, 'that was easier than I thought it would be. So let's talk now.'

'Don't wake the baby!' Gwen hissed. Always thinking of the baby. She stood awkwardly, wiping the back of her hand across her lips. 'Rhys! It's not what it looks like – well, OK, it's exactly what it looks like. But he just lunged at me! I didn't kiss back! Really, honestly, I didn't. He just kind of fell on me, just before you came through the door and... well, my reactions aren't what they were.'

'Neither's your sex drive, love,' I muttered bitterly.

'Hey!' she snapped, and I knew from how angry she was that she was utterly innocent. 'When he comes to, he'll tell you. One moment he was talking about how he and Sasha couldn't have kids and the next he lunged. Honest! I was really surprised.'

'And delighted!' I bellowed.

'Don't wake the baby,' repeated Gwen fiercely. She reached out to me, and I stepped back. 'Oh, come on, love,' she said. She was Reasoning With Me. I've always hated it when she does that. It means she's about to win using Logic. I hate you, Logic. 'Listen... Look at him. Skinny streak of piss in a shell suit! Rhys, you're almost old enough to be his dad. Do you really think... I mean, if I was going to cheat on you... which I never would... well, it wouldn't be with someone like that, would it, now?' And she looked at me, and her eyes were ever so wide and bright. 'Come on.'

'How did he kiss?' I asked.

She blinked, and then grinned. 'Bless him. It was like being rubbed by a hankie soaked in granny spit.'

I punched her lightly on the shoulder. She punched me back. We hugged.

'We OK?' she said, not letting me go. We walked around like contestants in a three-legged race. 'Are we OK?'

'Until I come home and find him naked on top of you. I'd love to hear your explanation for that one.'

'Oh, it'll be really good,' Gwen assured me seriously. 'And you'll buy it.'

'Sure I will,' I said, stroking her hair.

Gwen kicked out a foot. Davydd groaned. 'Oi, lover boy,' she said. 'You can stop pretending to be asleep. You need to get up and apologise.'

Davydd stood, looking tiny and scared. 'I'm sorry, mate,' he said. 'Mate' was an odd choice of word in the circumstances, but he went there, OK. 'I'm sorry

– but she's… she's wonderful.'

'Go home,' I said.

The door shut behind him with a rubber clunk.

'This is an odd place,' I said to Gwen.

She narrowed her eyes. 'Because a man finds me irresistibly attractive?'

'No,' I said, seriously. 'It's not that.'

Truth to tell a couple of other odd things happened later that week. I steered clear of Davydd as much as possible. But I'd noticed some of the women of the village still looking at me. If I didn't know better – and let's face it, I didn't – I would have sworn they were eyeing me up.

The cracker was when that leopard-print lass from the Y Gwyr saw me passing the bus stop with my pram. 'Hiya,' she said. By daylight she was even more *Hollyoaks Later* than I remembered. The least orange things about her were her teeth, which glowed a brilliant white as she worked gum around. Her eyes observed me. Casual. Hunting cat casual.

'What you doing down here, tiger? Anything special?' she asked, applying lip gloss over and over until I could see the sun in her smile.

'Oh, um, ah,' I managed. This wasn't going to be a great conversation. For some reason she had me on edge. I was mightily glad that Gwen wasn't around to watch me falling over my tongue. 'You know,' I continued, casually pushing down on the pram until the front wheels popped up. 'Shopping and stuff.'

'And stuff, eh?' She inclined her head slightly, and then carried on chewing while she worked through that thought. 'Fancy.' Another pause. 'I'm Nerys.'

Pretty much no one is called Nerys, and absolutely

not a girl in her early twenties who is mostly long legs and hair extensions. But she made it a bit sexy. She stuck out a hand and I shook it.

'Hello, Nerys, I'm Rhys.'

'I know.' She smirked, letting go of my hand slowly. 'Rhys spelt D-I-L-F. Rhys with the kid. Everyone knows about you. All us girls talk about you.' There was something like a wink.

OK, truth to tell, I may just have been flirting back with her, a really tiny little bit. It was a dull day, it was drizzling slightly and there I was being chatted up. I'm a man, all right, and I have manly urges. Although if you asked Gwen, she'd tell you my manly urges are farting in public and leaving the seat up. Shows how much she knows. 'And what are you up to, this fine day?' I asked. I did not add 'my pretty'. For Rhys Williams did not fall off the last train.

Nerys was heavy-lidded casual. 'I'm just waiting for a bus. It's my second favourite thing to do in a bus shelter.' Her eyebrows flared, then she looked down. It was a careful copy of Princess Diana doing demure. Mercifully, the lights of the approaching bus glowed round the corner, and it pulled up, the doors opening with a heartfelt sigh. Nerys leaned forward and breathed into my ear, 'Well, there's my ride,' then hopped on.

The bus chugged defiantly away up the hillside and I leaned back against the pram, exhaling for the longest time. 'Well, Anwen, love...' I was pleased. 'Daddy's still got it. Just saying.'

Of course, then it all stopped being fun and games.

Gwen

The bad day happened when I was out shopping. I went past the park, pushing the pram and listening to the glorious lack of noise from my lovely daughter. Other people's children were playing in the park, and I thought how nice it all looked – odd, but nice. All those lovely, black-haired kids running around. They were just so neat and quiet. Not like you'd expect 15-year-olds to be. No hoodies covered in fag ash and cider stains, no swearing, no music on their mobiles – just well-behaved, ordered play. Strangely blissful, if a little unusual. I couldn't wait till Anwen grew up to be like that. Patiently waiting her turn on the swings.

I spotted the policeman approaching and fought down the urge to panic. Odd that. I remembered when I was a copper and I'd walk up to a group – maybe just a gang hanging around when they should have been in school. Nothing spectacular. Just a nice, smiley young WPC all non-threatening body language and one of them would bolt, running like a scared hare. I'd think to myself (as I tried running after them in a body warmer) just what a stupid thing that was to do – guilt written all over their face. Dead giveaway. Never scarper. Always stand your ground.

Now I was on the other side of the tracks and the urge to flee was almost overwhelming. Of course, you can't really run with a pram. I mean, I'm sure they do it in LA as exercise, but what do I know?

Instead I planted my feet firmly where they were, smile on, eyes wide, baby toy ready. The innocent, innocent Earth Mother. I looked at him – typical friendly middle-aged Welsh bloke. Slightly gone-to-seed. Puffy skin, tired hair, massive bags under his eyes, but a confident strut to his stride. Oh yes, he was very pleased with himself. He raised an arm and waved. All hail-fare-and-well-met, god love him.

He approached. 'Mrs Williams?' he said, and may as well have bowed.

'Yes?' I said. Just at the moment I was going about under Rhys's name. We'd figured the whole hiding-in-plain-sight thing would be easier that way. After all, you couldn't have an alarm go off every time a couple called Williams moved into a Welsh village, could you now?

He stood there, rocking back on his feet and peering down into the pram. His face lit up like he'd seen an eclipse and for a moment he seemed utterly distracted.

'Can I help you, officer?' I asked and immediately fought the urge to bite my lip. *No one says that*, not unless you want to get on the list of the world's shiftiest people.

'Constable Brown,' he said, and looked very pleased about the fact. 'Call me Tony. Everyone does. What a beautiful child. Aw, we don't get many babies around here.' He smiled, making a little sausage-fingered baby wave down into the pram. Anwen ignored it, and I liked her all the more for it.

'Remarkable!' He straightened up. 'I was wondering if we could have the tiniest of chats?' His cordiality increased, one arm gesturing to a scabby park bench like it was a royal throne.

'Of course,' I said, feeling a bit sick. This could all be perfectly fine, after all. Just a routine enquiry. Actually, let's just pray he doesn't say that…

'Just a routine enquiry,' he said. Oh god. I perched uneasily on the mouldy, damp bench and he sat down next to me. A bit close, mind.

He pasted his hands across his knees, and then turned to me. Warm, friendly, patronising. 'What it is, see, well, it's a bit delicate…'

Oh, spit it out, love.

'We've had a report of an assault.'

'What?'

'Against Davydd Hope, you see,' he said.

'Ohhh…' I groaned.

'I see you know the man.' His whole face lit up like a smug fat light bulb. 'Good stuff, good stuff. And would you be able, perhaps, to talk about the incident I might be referring to?'

'When he suddenly kissed me?' I asked.

He sucked air through his teeth. 'I'm not interested in your private life, Mrs Williams. But I do want to know about your husband's reaction…' He attempted a delicate cough. It was all a bit pantomime, if you ask me. But underneath it all, sharp white teeth. He edged a little nearer, hitched up his lips, flashed a bit more gum.

I decided to play it dead straight. 'Oh, what when Rhys lamped him one? Too bloody right! What would you have done, Tony?'

Constable Brown managed an actual not-for-me-to-say harrumph.

'Oh, come on.' I warmed up. 'He was livid! And

the boy deserved a smack! He just launched himself on me as Rhys walked in. What would you do if you found your wife snogging another man...?'

He looked like he was considering my words, carefully and interestedly. 'Indeed, indeed. Tricky. It is a delicate situation. Poor Davydd is a nice enough lad, but a bit troubled... But I was very keen to seek you out. To get your side of the story. To meet the woman who could drive him to such extremes of passion, you might say. You're quite the Helen of our fair Parish, Mrs Williams, really you are. Quite the floater of boats! What a treat for the eyes!' He laughed his jolly little laugh and squinted at me. I tried to read what was going on behind his eyes, but not well enough. 'Poor Davydd is somewhat shamefaced about his actions, obviously, and I'm sure we all think it would be a shame if this went any further. A dreadful shame.' He smiled a big smile. All friends together.

'So he's not pressing charges?'

'Oh, I didn't say that, now,' huffed Constable Brown, all outraged dignity. 'I just said...' He slowed down, and looked at me, then glanced across at Anwen. 'Is she yours?' he asked, suddenly.

I was a bit startled. 'Yes! Of course she is!'

'The local celebrity, she is.' He sucked his teeth. 'Forgive me, Mrs Williams. Gwen. Stupid thing to say. But it's nice to know. And a pleasure to meet her mother. A real treat.' His voice dropped, and his complacent smile suddenly became something else. Something odd. It was a look I couldn't quite... couldn't quite pin down.

'As I said,' he continued haltingly, a little flushed, 'you are a wonderful mother. And these misunderstandings can get so unpleasant. So very difficult. I'm sure we're all keen to avoid that. In whatever way we can...' His hand, grasping the bench, flexed and unflexed, and then landed on my leg, gripping it firmly, pinching the flesh.

I gasped and made to move, but he slid in quick and close, his face red and leering. All trace of the genial village bobby was gone, and this was a snarling, wild beast. I started to cry out, but all I could hear as he pressed down on me was his voice whispering, 'Beautiful mother! As soon as I saw you I thought, oh yes, I'll have some of that...'

Oh my god. Not in a dark alleyway on my way home after a club. But here. In broad daylight in a kids' playground.

I reached up to fight him off, but he was gripping both my arms tightly. I called out, but first his fat salty fingers, then his dreadful mouth pushed down on mine. My eyes twisted around to try and see anyone, but the pram, the bloody pram was blocking me from view.

I tried headbutting him, but he jerked to one side, biting down on my lip, still laughing. No sodding strength. Bloody beached-whale Gwen. Unable to fight back. I looked up, pleading at the leering face above me. Please god, I thought. Please let this not be happening... somehow make it stop...

And then he tumbled to the floor with a groan. Standing over him were the three kids from the park, their black hair shining in the feeble sun.

'Was this man annoying you?' one of them asked, a pretty, horse-faced boy of about 15. I looked again. They were all pretty, horse-faced boys of about 15. Like brothers.

Two of them reached out, helping me up. 'I am Peter,' said the other one, taking a firm grasp on the pram. 'Come along,' he said, 'You must be disturbed. We will take you to mother.'

Rhys

It took me about twenty minutes to get there.

A kid came to get me, knocking at the silly little door until I opened it, bleary-eyed.

'Good afternoon. It is about your wife,' he said, his face serious. 'She is well, but you should come.'

'What's up?' I asked.

He started to tell me.

I got very angry.

He kept on repeating that Gwen was fine, but I'm not sure I heard it. I was dizzy, sick and red angry. I ran from the caravan park, out through the lane, down into the village. My head flying with furious thoughts and threats and rash promises. When I got to the right house, a kid opened the door. Didn't notice him, sorry.

After the event, I'd say he was another of the square children from the village – you know, dark hair, slightly old-fashioned clothes, plain look. Typical. Straightforward. But I barged past him, thundering along the hallway with its tired carpet and vinyl runner, and through the smoked-glass door into the kitchen, one of those old kitchens, you know the kind – welsh dresser, oil cloth, chipped mugs and lino. As soon as I entered, Mrs Harries appeared, handing me a cup of tea, but I didn't even notice. I was here for Gwen.

She was sat in a chair by the electric fire – all

three bars were turned on, so she was obviously royalty. Anwen was pressed to her, and Gwen smiled at me, the same tired smile she threw on after she'd given birth. She looked almost as dazed. She'd been crying – I could tell.

I hugged her, spilt a bit of tea, and hugged her again.

She shushed me. 'It's OK, Rhys, nothing really happened. It's all OK. Peter stopped it.'

'Peter?'

The boy who'd fetched me stepped forward and nodded. 'Your wife did not seem happy.'

'Too bloody right, she didn't,' I growled. 'Thank you.'

She talked a bit more about what had gone on. Mrs Harries made more tea and listened.

'I don't get it,' I said. 'I mean, I just don't get it.' I stood up. 'I'm going to find that man, and I'm going to knock his block off. Then I'm going to ask him why he did that to you.'

'Rhys…' began Gwen.

The boy Peter looked at me. 'Because of us,' he said simply.

Mrs Harries pushed back the curls of her grey hair and leaned forward, tapping me on the wrist gently. 'Have a seat, dear,' she said, her voice patient and warm.

She was one of those women who looked perfectly fifty. In a way that you could never imagine her being younger, with long blonde hair and wearing a dress without any flowers on it. No, age suited her. Everything about her said freshly baked cakes and Tupperware and lots of tea. She sat down comfortably on a pine kitchen chair opposite me, and topped up my mug, and as she did so, the light in her eyes went. Suddenly, she looked ever so sad.

'It's to do with the children,' she said.

Megan Harries

It was in 1987 that it all went wrong. We never knew why, really. But it was about then. Something in the water – perhaps due to mining, maybe Chernobyl, someone said. But the births stopped.

The government sent out some people – they had a good look round. You know the kind – flash-looking, suits, dark glasses, but none of them ever said who they were. They weren't the first, they weren't the last. People came to Rawbone and they made encouraging noises and they went away.

But they never got to the bottom of it. There was something wrong with the people of Rawbone. None of us could see a child through to term. Every now and then, one of us girls would get pregnant, and the rest of us would all pretend happiness while seething with jealousy and then a secret, awful sad triumph went it all came to nothing.

The government sent us special doctors, and we were well looked after, I'll say that for them. A few of the men of the village went away, tried to have kids elsewhere, but they couldn't. A few women moved away too, but nothing came of that either. Everyone drifted back. We were all stuck here, glued together by our shameful secret. We didn't tell anyone. We just… couldn't bear the world looking at us.

It wasn't like Thalidomide or anything like that – no one could see what was causing it. There were grumblings that it was the government, but all the people who came out here were ever so nice. So straightforward and honest and sad for us.

Some of the men here said it was the old airbase and marched on it – well, it was the 1980s. They went there, they broke down the fence, they marched around... but there was really very little there. Just a few old planes, a lighthouse and a lot of birds' mess. No nuclear warheads or anything.

It was just a mystery. No one knew what was behind it. No one seemed to care. Then one day, we were called to a meeting in the town hall. The whole village. A man in an army greatcoat said that there was something they could do for us after all... He said, what with the mark hanging over the village, they couldn't let us adopt in case we passed it on to others, but they could... well, they were willing to give us what they called the Next Best Thing. Something new.

And that's when these children started turning up. It's like they came in the night along with the milk. You just had to let them know that you wanted a child and you'd find one, sat cross-legged on the doorstep in the morning. Patient and kind.

They're called Scions. We were told they weren't quite like normal children. Not in a good way or a bad way – just in their way. They don't grow up. They're just the same as when they turned up. Mine all look about 15, more or less, although I've had them a good few years apart. First Paul. Then Peter. Jenny's not actually mine, but she hangs around here a lot. Her mother runs the shop – Mrs Meredith, nice lady but she and Jenny don't really see eye to eye. Jenny's one of the oldest Scions. Proof that they don't really change. They're so neat, and so kind and polite. Always. They never argue, or make any fuss, or cause trouble. They're just there.

The next best thing.

Rhys

'But what do you mean?' I asked.

Mrs Harries rested her hand on her teacup. 'They're well meaning. They're just a bit too perfect. Sorry, my dears,' she said.

The three children stood over her. Patient, kind. Placid. And suddenly just a bit unnerving. 'That's all right, mother,' said Peter.

'What are you?' gasped Gwen.

'We are Scions. That's all we know,' said Peter.

'We are here to be children,' said Jenny.

'Is there anything else we can help you with?' asked the other.

'Are you... are you aliens?' I asked.

Jenny shrugged. 'We do not know. We only know that we are Scions. That we love our parents and must obey them.'

Whoa. Majorly creepy. Didn't help that she was considering me with her strangely empty porcelain doll stare. There was the tiny hint of something in her gaze – she was in on a joke that I wouldn't get.

Mrs Harries made to lay a hand on Gwen, but stopped as Gwen flinched. 'Sorry, my dear. It's your coming here... You see, there's never been a proper child here since that time. Sasha, Davydd and Nerys were the last births in the village. And, after that, well, we just stopped having outsiders around. The caravan park shut down. And those of us with family outside... somehow they knew we were tainted – they didn't bring their children with them to stay, or invite us to visit. We were cursed. We can take a hint. We don't exactly seek out others. Only a couple of buses stop here. We're not on the way to anywhere. So we've been... isolated. But to see you, all of a sudden, the two of you, with a baby... it's had an odd effect on us all. Shaken us up a bit... I had hoped it would be a good thing. It's certainly reminded me of what we've lost. I know that people here are seeing in you and Rhys... well, hoping that maybe one of you can solve their situation. Can give them a child of their own.'

'Oh my god,' said Gwen.

I remembered Nerys at the bus shelter, and groaned.

'Yes,' Mrs Harries rested her hand on Gwen's, and this time she didn't flinch.

We didn't talk on the walk back home. It was raining heavily, and Gwen was wrapped up like a squaw, as though she didn't want the world to see her.

The whole world seemed awful. Even the stink thistles were drooping their heads glumly.

Never before had that grim little caravan seemed like home. But it seemed safe, a refuge. Gwen flopped down in that horrible chair and started to feed Anwen, fussing over her socks, and changing her little baby T-shirt over and over again. She didn't seem to be listening to me.

'Right.' I'd had enough. 'Come on, we're packing up and we're getting out of here. Right now.'

'No.' Gwen didn't look up from the baby. In the old days, her voice would have been firm, loud and spoiling for a fight. Now it was just hollow and deeply tired.

'Are you kidding?' I yelled.

Gwen pressed a hand to her head. 'Just put the kettle on, love.'

I boiled the kettle.

We sat and had tea.

After a while, Gwen broke the silence. 'I'd kill for something stronger.'

'Yeah,' I agreed.

We sipped our tea and watched the rain.

I stood up, trotted over to the kitchen drawer and pulled out the sheaf of takeaway menus we'd miraculously acquired. 'I'm getting us a pizza and some beer,' I said.

Gwen made that 'ooh' noise she used to make when she'd soak her feet after a day on the beat. I switched my mobile on. For once, the tiniest bit of signal. I rang one firm. Then another. Then I started to shout.

'What is the point in giving us the bloody leaflets if you don't deliver?' A pause. 'I see. Well, yes, but I've had a really bad day and I don't feel like coming in to collect it. No. No. Thank you.' And I might have shouted some more. But I'm leaving that out.

I slammed down the phone. Well, you can't really slam a mobile. I kind of tossed it across the counter. But not too hard. Didn't want to break it. Not when we were about an hour's drive from the nearest greasy-child-in-a-tie phone store.

'Lovely,' said Gwen. 'I'm trapped in a caravan with two babies.'

'Don't worry,' I told her. 'I'll pop to the petrol station and get us something.'

'No.' Gwen grabbed my hand, needy. Gwen was *never* needy. 'Don't. Please don't leave me.'

I looked at her.

'Oh god, love.' I wrapped her in a hug. As much of a hug as was possible without squeezing our baby into jam.

'This feels so good,' she laughed. 'Like old times.'

'Yeah,' I breathed. 'You OK?'

'No,' she said.

'I won't ever let you go.'

'Actually, you'd better,' sighed Gwen. 'Anwen's just sicked up something.'

'Right.'

Cleaned and tidied and with two tins of spaghetti on the go, we looked at each other.

'I was nearly…' Gwen swallowed. 'No, not using the word.'

'What are we going to do about it?'

'We can hardly call the police, can we, now?'

'Good point. I can go round there later and…'

'No,' said Gwen.

I shook my head. I felt so outraged. So furious and sick. Still. I checked my hand. It was shaking. God knew how Gwen was coping.

'Right then,' I said. 'Well at least we know why Ianto had keys to this place. Is there any escape from your old life? From bloody Torchwood?'

'No,' admitted Gwen. 'We just keep moving.'

'Is that what we do, then? We move on? Pack up tonight, pick another key and pray?'

'It could be worse.'

'OK,' I sighed. 'I'll pack after we've had hoops.'

'No.' Gwen's eyes were wide. 'I meant the

next place could be worse. Worse than this one. If Torchwood had keys to these places it means there's unfinished business in all of them. I think we should stay.'

'But…' I protested, 'this place is so sad.'

'Yeah,' sighed Gwen. 'Yes it is.' She brightened. 'Let's find out why.'

Gwen

We talked what we were going to do about it for a bit, in between spooning hoops from the bowl and feeding and changing Anwen. We talked until I could feel my eyelids snapping shut.

All those little hints of my old life that I'd never get away from. I could outrun Men in Black, but not my past. I wondered how fair it was to drag Rhys along with me. That nice, sexy bloke I'd met once, so very long ago. In those days it was spaghetti bolognese, cooked from scratch with ingredients sourced from only the finest 24-hour shop. Now two sad little value tins tipped into a saucepan decorated with rustic hens was all we had time for.

I watched him stirring the thin sauce dourly, my sexy man who hated being put on hold and loved things that ran on time. Who liked order, routine, beer and predictability. I'd taken all that from him, piece by piece. Here we were, in the middle of bloody nowhere. None of his old friends to talk to, not Banana Boat or Lottery Dave. No one.

Just me. And the child. And neither of us were great company.

Oh, Rhys, what have I done to you? You can take the man out of the fun, but can you take the fun out of the man? Looks like I've tried bloody hard.

Just me. I've left so much behind. All those friends of mine. The girls I'd go out on the lash with.

Ianto. Tosh. Owen. Jack. Andy. They say it happens when you get pregnant – you stop meeting up with people quite so much. You give up your friends along with the booze except for the odd not-taking-it-too-seriously-glass. In your head you're thinking that, once you've had the baby, it'll all be back to normal. In a bit. Honest.

I'd been expecting we'd just spend a bit too much time alone in the flat, or breastfeeding over tea in John Lewis. Not that we'd be trapped in a caravan park. With our friends dead or millions of light years away. And us utterly unable to escape.

I saw Constable Tony Brown's face pressing down on me. I shook my head. No. Not yet, Gwen love. Not yet.

I thought of all the things Mrs Harries had said. Rhys and I argued them back and forth. All those hints and clues of my old life – those bloody odd kids. What were they? What were we going to do? What about that mention of a man in a military greatcoat? There was only one person that could be... Surely?

'There's a thing we've forgotten.' Rhys had adopted that 'seriously' tone he sometimes used. Normally before suggesting we redecorate or try a detox.

'Oh yes?' I was guarded.

'They talked about an abandoned airbase.'

'Oh,' I said. 'I see what you mean.'

His face lit up. 'Glad you do. I've no bloody idea what it means, just that... that it sounds...'

'It does, doesn't it?' I agreed. 'Like a sore thumb.'

I yawned. 'But I'm dead on my arse. I am flat-out knackered. I would kill for two hours' sleep.'

Rhys chuckled. 'If you could only hear yourself.'

'Oh, I know. I know.' I rolled my eyes. 'Listen to us.

Trying to solve a mystery when I'm too tired to even open a jar. Talking of which, better bring over the expresso bongo. Let's top up madam's milk supply so you can feed her while I crash.'

So much to do these days before you go to sleep. In the old days it'd be throw your keys down, grab a glass of water as you flung your shoes off into the far corners and then fall onto your pillow. Not now. Now it was like I had a to-do list so long I may as well have given up on ever getting it done.

So there I was, yawning helplessly, with the expresser pump clamped to a breast when there was a knock at the door.

'Oh god,' I thought sickly. Let it not be bloody Tony Brown.

'I'll get it.' Rhys managed a tone that was both firm and warning. My hero.

He went to open the door.

Rhys

I opened the door. Tom and Josh stood there in the rain, both wearing bright yellow windcheaters. They looked like wet Teletubbies.

'Hello,' said Tom. 'Megan Harries gave us a call. Can we come in?'

'We've brought beer,' smiled Josh. 'And pizza.'

'Let 'em in,' yelled Gwen.

They came in and sat down, and suddenly our little mobile home felt crowded.

They did all the right things. They asked Gwen how she was and didn't take her first reply as an answer. They fussed around. Redheaded Tom tidied the kitchen a bit, rinsed out the tins, served up the pizza and made loud chit-chat. Josh played with Anwen.

Josh pushed the steaming box of pizza at Gwen. Tom curled up next to him, letting Josh do all the talking while he did the eating. That's pretty much how it is in most relationships. There's always an eater.

Gwen picked away at a slice.

'Oh go on.' Josh frowned at her. 'It's safe. It's covered in prawns, stilton and peanuts.'

'Sod off,' laughed Gwen, and wolfed down a slice. She sipped a little of my beer and belched.

'Gwen!' I protested, secretly delighted at how much happier she seemed.

'Sod off too,' she growled. 'I've had a bloody awful day.'

'So,' I said. I had to reassert my authority. 'What are we going to do about the assault?'

Josh blinked. I suddenly got it. I understood Rawbone. It was a place where no one ever called a spade a spade. That's how it got by. It made compromises, avoided any awkward words, never quite met anyone in the eye. Even, let's face it, Josh and Tom. I'm fairly sure they'd never actually said they were your actual gays. They'd never even used the word, or any word – 'partner', 'other half'. I got the feeling it was just another issue for the whole village to dodge. Maybe they referred to each other as 'friends' with just the tiniest of pauses. A whole village of small domestic secrets. It seemed like the perfect place to come when you were on the run.

'Come on, mate,' I pressed on. 'What do we do?'

Josh shifted uncomfortably. 'I shouldn't worry about it.'

Tom glanced at him then, sharply, but I'd already started shouting.

Anwen made a noise, so I stopped shouting. In the uneasy, snuffling silence, Gwen reached out, pointing the tip of her pizza at Josh. 'Ignore him. Why shouldn't we worry about it?'

'This village...' said Josh. 'It's not normal. You must know that by now. It'll be taken care of.'

'I see,' Gwen nodded. 'You know there's something not right about the village, don't you?'

'How could we not?' laughed Josh. 'We bloody live here.'

Tom looked like he was about to say something, and then reached for another slice of pizza. There was already sauce on his T-shirt and a bit of onion on the carpet. Josh, however, remained immaculate, picking away at a single slice.

'What made you move here?' asked Gwen.

'Oh, work.' Tom shrugged. 'You know how it is.'

'But,' pressed Gwen, and I realised that she was still sixty-seven per cent copper, 'you know about the children, don't you?'

'Yeah.' Tom stared glumly at his pizza.

'None of our business.' Josh smiled. It was an interesting smile. You know when you're off to see your GP and they're leafing through their paperwork and they flash you a smile before they tell you there's nothing particular to worry about, but... Or you're getting the car MOT'd and the man at the garage wipes his oily hands down on his overalls and then smiles before he breaks the bad news... That kind of smile. Like he didn't want to be drawn into a long discussion of the particulars. 'Seriously, why should we care about kids? They're not even sexy, not even in a Tom Daley Wrong way.'

Gwen blinked.

'What? Oh, he *is*,' continued Josh. 'We've got a cat. That's enough. Kids are horrible things. No offence.'

'None taken,' I said, pulling away at the bottle of beer. It felt bloody gorgeous.

'I mean, I'm sure yours is great,' Tom covered, pointlessly and nervously.

'But...' Gwen again, not letting the original subject go. 'The children. The children here are wrong.'

'Aren't they?' said Josh. 'But it's not our business. It really isn't. If it makes everyone else here happy. If it lets them get on with their lives... who are we to interfere?'

Tom nodded.

'Live and let live, eh?' Josh trotted out that smile again. 'I mean, it has its advantages. They don't seem that fussed about having an Indian hairdresser living in town. And no one is asking what the two of you are doing here. As I said, it has its advantages.'

BANG. Payload dropped. The gentlest of threats. Don't rock the boat. Please don't rock the boat.

Then Tom pushed another bottle of beer across the table towards Gwen. All friends again.

'Hey,' Gwen protested. 'I've only drunk half and I'm tiddly.'

'Get tiddlier.' Josh pressed the bottle on Gwen. 'We'd have brought gin, but isn't that wrong for mums?'

'Trust me,' sighed Gwen. 'You'd be about nine months late with that one. And don't worry – *everything* is wrong for mums. Thanks, by the way.'

'For what?' asked Josh. 'It was Tom's idea.' Tom looked uncomfortable at that, but Josh pressed on: 'For coming over in your hour of need?'

'No.' Gwen swigged at the beer. 'For not offering me advice on breastfeeding.'

'Ah well,' said Tom. 'We don't care. Everyone else though... everyone's very pleased. Fascinated. And they've all got an opinion.'

'Everyone has,' sighed Gwen. 'I think it's worse here than it would be in Cardiff. There it'd be, "And when you gonna have another one, Gwen dear?"'

'We're not having another baby, are we?' I asked, suddenly alarmed.

'Trust me –' Gwen narrowed her eyes – 'it'll be a long time before I let you near me again, Rhys Williams.'

And everyone laughed. Everyone else laughed.

We sat, talking and giggling, and suddenly life didn't seem so miserable. It felt normal and easy again. True, Anwen woke up a couple of times and had to be changed once, but it was almost like... normal life.

But ticking away, underneath it all, were Josh's guarded smile and Gwen's brain. Someone had switched it to 'investigation', and away it was going.

'So,' she said, all wide-eyed and casual, 'someone said something about there being an airbase. Which means lots of nice men in uniform, doesn't it? Do you two boys know anything about it?'

'Yeah,' said Josh, playing his card. 'Tom works there.'

Oh.

Gwen

I stared at Tom. Hard. He swallowed. The slice of pizza hung limp in his hand.

'You work there?'

He giggled, nervously, and ran a hand through his tightly curled red hair. 'Well, it's not actually an airbase as such. It's really a Weather Monitoring Station.'

'Right,' I said dourly.

Rhys guffawed.

Josh smirked.

'Stop it!' protested Tom. 'It really is! It does monitor the weather.'

'It's Wales,' I pointed out. 'It's raining. What do you do with the rest of the day?'

Tom muttered very quietly.

'He really can't say,' whispered Josh, holding a finger to his lips. 'Even I don't know exactly. Not that it's top secret. Oh no. Although if it were, he wouldn't be able to say that.'

'Shaddup,' growled Tom, kicking him. 'I'm a meteorologist. Really.'

'He really is.' Josh leaned forward and helped himself to another beer.

I joined in the laughter. 'Yeah, but come on… It's got to be a military base of some kind?'

'It is a monitoring station,' repeated Tom.

'Monitoring the kids?' I asked.

Tom wouldn't say any more. He was clearly hiding something. But that was all I was going to get out of them. For the moment. There was that little tell-tale feeling in the air, like there was more to come. I'd get it out of them, sooner or later.

We drank some more, finished the pizza and then Josh stood up. 'Right, this is where we love you and leave you.' He yawned. 'We're walking home through the rain. You guys can get some top-notch zizzing in.'

As he stepped out into the rain, Tom murmured, 'Hope you're feeling a bit better.'

I shrugged. I didn't really know. I said I'd be fine.

They walked away. I leaned on Rhys. 'I've had two whole bottles of beer,' I giggled. 'I feel all warm and squidgy.'

'Hey-ho,' he sighed. 'I married a lightweight.'

'Has its advantages,' I said.

'Oh. Right.'

In the middle of the night, Rhys got out of bed to feed the baby. He was gone a long time, and I missed him.

I dreamed again. I dreamed I was in a big grey building surrounded by body bags, all of them a strange, cheery shade of red.

I crossed the hall, my footsteps echoing on the lino, marked out for ball games. They led me, not quite at gunpoint, towards two body bags.

My friends, Jack and Ianto, had died trying to save us all.

I unzipped the bags and looked at their faces, oddly alike in death. Both of them looked strangely peaceful, as though glad of a rest.

But I knew that at any moment, one of them was going to wake up. Jack Harkness would sit bolt upright, gasping for air. For a moment, he'd smile, relieved to see me, and then he'd remember, remember that Ianto was never going to open his eyes again.

Then we'd realise we had no idea what to say, so we'd just hold each other, looking down at the body of Ianto Jones, lying there in that great big grim sports hall.

Only this time, in the dream, I waited ever such a long while and neither of them came back to life.

Rhys

I stood in the road throwing stones at the police station. I was angry. I was also feeling a little stupid. It was a tiny little building – like a suburban two-up-two-down, with a cop shop in the living room and a small flat upstairs. I'd tried hammering on the door. I didn't really know why I was there, but I did know that I wanted to hit PC Tony Brown quite a lot until I stopped shaking.

But the bloody door wouldn't open. So I was throwing gravel at the window and shouting.

A hand touched me lightly on the shoulder.

'Gah!' I gasped, startled.

It was one of the Scions. A girl. She was just standing there, at three o'clock in the morning.

She spoke. 'Good morning.' Her voice was completely flat. 'What are you doing?'

'Hello,' I said. 'It's Jenny, isn't it?'

'Yes,' she agreed.

'What are you doing up at this hour?'

She considered the question. 'I have not acquired the habit of sleeping.' She shrugged. 'So I walk. My mother does not like it. It rains at night. My clothes get wet. My mother says I will catch cold.' A sudden slyness came in. 'But I do not catch colds.' A pause. 'What are you doing?'

'Trying to wake up a policeman.'

'Have you phoned 999?' she asked.

'No.'

'That is what you are supposed to do,' she confided.

'Not in this case. This is private.'

'I understand. Would you like to see the Police Constable?'

'Bloody right I would.'

Jenny strode forward and looked at the frosted glass door. 'You have tried knocking?'

'Yes.' I was impatient, desperately hoping she'd go away.

'Do you think he is hurt?'

'Hope so.'

'Then he could be in trouble?'

'Heaps.'

'Heaps.' Jenny repeated the word, considering this. While she did it, she twisted the door knob. The lock made a sudden pop and the door swung open. 'There,' she announced. 'I am strong.'

I looked at the door. And wondered what to do. What to do. This was mad.

'Would you like me to come with you?' she asked.

'No,' I said. I made up my mind. 'No. Thank you. Can you run along home now?

She nodded. 'I can.' But she didn't move.

Not labouring the point, but the whole situation was a bit creepy. A bit? A lot.

Jenny was nice. She was helpful. But there was also something utterly, utterly wrong about her. Just standing there in the 3 a.m. drizzle. Placid. Unconcerned. A mannequin. I remembered Mrs Harries's words. There was something not quite right about the children. Jenny stood there, her long locks impossibly neat around her. Her face mildly interested. Unconcerned.

I stepped towards the doorway, but a movement beyond startled me. The door swung open and a man stood there. Dishevelled. Bleary. Tired. Drunk. He blinked at me.

'Ohhhh…' he said.

I hit him.

I was a bit surprised by that. But it was absolutely the right thing to do. The odd thing is he didn't fight back, he just dropped like a stone. I stood there. Feeling a bit odd. Like, what did I do now?

I realised he was crying. A large, ugly man curled up and sobbing.

'I'm sorry,' he bleated. His voice was wet and snotty. He didn't seem anything other than pathetic. 'I am so sorry.'

Jenny stepped forward, interested. 'Why is Mr Brown sad? Why are you hitting him?'

'Because he's an arsehole,' I said.

Brown looked up. Not at me, but at the child. And he flinched. 'What are you doing here?' he shouted.

'Watching,' Jenny replied. 'You are sad and injured. Why is this?'

'Because of you!' he snarled, suddenly, leaping up, tottering on his feet. 'You! This is what you've… you…' He stopped and leaned back against a wall, sinking slightly. His breath wafted over to me, a drunk's tangle of beer and spirits. He started crying again, wiping a hand across his eyes. 'I am so sorry.' His voice was thick with self-pity. 'You don't know… You don't know what it's like… You don't understand.'

'No, no I don't. What were you trying to do to my wife?' I said.

He stopped, mid snivel. 'I only wanted... I wanted a *cwtch*, a cuddle.' He went quiet. *Cuddle*. It's one of those words, isn't it? It's a bit Hallmark at the best of times. But it really didn't fit what he'd tried to do to Gwen.

As though sensing my rage boiling up again, Jenny stepped forward hurriedly. 'You are lonely?' she asked him, her face curious.

Tony didn't look at the child, but carried on speaking, deflating with every word. 'You just don't get it, do you, mate? You don't know what this place is like. There's no escape. There is no hope here... But your wife. She is so beautiful. She's a proper woman. A real woman. She's... ripe.'

I hit him again. It seemed the right thing to do. Again.

Jenny blinked with surprise.

He stood up after that, trying to straighten himself out. I suddenly realised how beefy and strong he was when he stood up to his full height. A meaty plate of a hand landed gently on my shoulder. 'Strictly speaking,' he said, his voice thick with booze and exhaustion, 'you shouldn't hit a policeman.' He smiled a crooked smile. 'But I bloody deserve it. I... I just... She was there and she was so... You only realise what's missing when you suddenly see the real thing.' He shook his head. 'Is she OK?'

'No,' I said.

'Right,' he nodded. Then he groaned and started to cry again, grizzling away. 'What have I done?' He swung back to Jenny. 'What have you made me do?'

'I have made you do nothing,' she seemed puzzled.

Tony stumbled forward. We were both standing

on his porch, in the damp and the freezing cold. He was wearing a rumpled T-shirt and a bloody hideous pair of boxer shorts. He looked pathetic. Utterly. His bunched hand pointed at the girl.

'You... you remind me that this place...' he slurred, repeating himself. 'This place is so wrong. That we are wrong. And every bloody day we have to look at you. The best thing we can manage.' He took another step towards her, and then, with a sudden snarl, lashed out.

Jenny didn't blink. She just reached out with a hand, closing on his wrist. 'Mrs Harries says I am not to let other people hit me,' she announced. Tony gave a yell as she turned her hand slightly and his arm twisted a little wrong. Then she let go.

Tony crumpled back against his front door. 'See?' he hissed at me. 'See? What kind of a bloody child is that?' He cradled his arm in his other hand. 'You've broken my arm!' he wailed.

'No more than you deserve, mate,' I said, feeling a terrible satisfaction.

'I have not broken your arm,' said Jenny. 'There is merely mild tearing in the rotator cuff. That is all.'

The policeman swore at her, straightening unsteadily. 'I need a bloody drink,' he announced, wobbling back inside. 'You want one?' he asked, with a woozy kind of hospitality.

'No.'

'No thank you,' said Jenny politely.

'I wasn't asking you,' snapped Tony. His paw wiped at the sweat on his brow as he frowned, staring and thinking and staring some more. 'What a bloody mess, eh? Think I'd better go back to bed. Look, are we done? Are we OK?'

'Don't come near my wife again.' I couldn't think what else to say. There are situations where even the best words you can come up with are a bit lame.

He smiled a little. 'I couldn't. I just couldn't. You are such a lucky man. She is perfect.'

'Yeah,' I said. 'She bloody is.'

'I am so sorry.' His voice had become a whine. 'I am so sorry for what I've done.' He vanished inside his house and started to crawl up the stairs like an old dog.

'Shall I close the door?' asked Jenny.

I shrugged, indifferent.

'Do you still wish to make sure that he is all right?'

'No,' I said. 'I'm going home.'

'I see,' she replied. 'I shall continue to walk. There are still two and a half hours until my mother wakes up. I may go and pick some flowers.'

'Right then,' I said, 'Good night.'

'Yes,' she said. I walked away. She stood there in the rain. Her eyes open. I couldn't tell if she was watching me or not.

Gwen was still fast asleep. Anwen stirred slightly in her cot. She made a noise that could have meant *Is that you, Daddy?* or *Is there food?*

'Hush,' I said, lifting her up, ever so gently. 'Let's not wake Mum, eh?' I went to the fridge and gave her some milk. Then I plonked her back in the cot and settled down in the chair, staring at her through the bars. She looked so peaceful, so innocent, her little tiny baby snores the only sound in the world.

I fell asleep.

Eloise

So, another shitty day at work.

Tom was hung over, which was a great help.
He sat there, cradling a 'World's Worst Boss' mug.
Some toast was on the table next to him, along with
a game on his phone that was commanding most of
his attention. In front of him, the massed processors
of the monitoring station churned away, performing
countless thousands of computations a second. And
the only screen he was looking at was a gossip site
about Angelina Jolie.

'Hey!' he called. Even his hair was hung over, the
curl quite gone.

'Rough night?' I asked.

'Oh, nothing deadly,' he assured me. 'Just a little
bit full of beer and pizza. But all in a good cause.
Listen, there's something I need to talk to you
about...'

'Is it about Angelina? Is she adopting another
orphan?'

'No, it's actually quite different.'

Then Sebastian came in. Sebastian is as unlike
Tom as you could hope for. Sebastian is younger,
and altogether more efficient. Tom was sat there in
a rumpled-yet-fashionable T-shirt, pale, interesting,
bored. Sebastian was wearing a suit. I've told him
there's really no need, but he insists. He says he
likes it. He always greets me in the morning with a

freshly made coffee.

When you're from Seattle, you grow up to appreciate a good cup of coffee. Of course, there is no such thing as a good cup of coffee in Wales. Scratch that. There is no such thing as a good cup of coffee in Great Britain. I sometimes wonder if it's the water, or if they just don't quite get it. But it's like they've all missed a memo. Or just want you drink more tea.

Sebastian, however, really gets coffee. I don't know what we'd do without him. We're lucky to have him.

He also does most of the work. Tom, sadly, is mostly window dressing. Pretty window dressing. But all the same.

It's odd, but there I was in the middle of bloody nowhere, working with two men who could probably get work as male models. When I was young, I always wanted to work abroad. Somewhere exciting and foreign. I never dreamt it would be Wales. But there I was, and the work was utterly fascinating.

The whole idea of a controlled village was just... I mean, clearly it occasionally gave me the ethical heebie-jeebies. But the Scions were the best hope these poor people had. It's fascinating, and at the same time just utterly thunder-facing. The nice thing about Sebastian and Tom is that they don't challenge me morally. Sebastian agrees with me, and Tom doesn't really care. He just likes the work. Well, the pretty much total lack of work.

I wander through the office, past the banks of frankly so-obsolete-it's-ha-ha-funny computer terminals. They're still working. Still watching. Still whirring away. Over the years we've brought in new systems, but we've not taken away the old ones. They're still there.

The thing is... stuff was robust back then. When NASA launched their *Voyager* probes, they were expecting the things to be a joy for a fortnight – but they're still going over thirty years later, still beaming back to us from the fringes of the solar system.

It's like that with these computers. I may own a more intelligent hairdryer, but those beauties belonged to an era where you designed a computer for a single purpose and built it to last. These old girls just sit there, churning away, each one with an elephantine carbon footprint (actually, what is the carbon footprint of elephants?), but still, after thirty years, doing their duty. Sentinels. Keeping watch.

I paused at the door of my office. I'd have loved nothing more than to go down to the hangar that morning. Every morning. The hangar always felt like proper work. Real and genuine 'frontiers-of-science' stuff. Whereas my office was... oh, if it wasn't emails it was database tables, spreadsheets, forecasts and answering questions I've answered countless times before.

My PC was already on. Sebastian always boots it up for me every morning. He's just being helpful, but it simply means that my inbox is staring at me, waiting. Like a boring, pitiless eye.

And there it was. An email from Jasmine.

I remember my first meeting with her. It's the only time I'd ever actually seen her. She pretty much met me off the plane. Trouser suit. Always a bad sign. Delighted I had come over, lucky to have me, it would be a privilege, she'd be very hands-off but always fight my corner, nod-nod-nod, open smile, warm body language. Clearly, I thought, she's been on a lot of courses.

Mind you, what a poetic name, I thought. Turns out it was the only poetic thing about her. Of course, she was really a corporal or something. So she was actually Corp. J. Bailey. Maybe having such a sweet name is what made her decide to become a trained killing machine. Anyhow, it was a quick meet-and-greet and then she packed us onto the six-hour train journey here, almost before I'd had a chance to take a picture of the London Eye or the Palace or anything much really. Slicing out of London on a giant modern train. Then changing at Wolverhampton (don't ask) onto a smaller and grubbier train that smelt of dog. Then changing again at a place with a name that was mostly 'Ms', 'Y's and 'DD's onto a couple of damp carriages that took forever to rattle along some breathtakingly grey coast. Wales is so damn beautiful, but I wonder what it would look like if they ever turned on the sun?

By Wolverhampton, Jasmine and I had already run out of things to say to each other. I tried pulling out some of my notes, but she frowned at me. Clearly, too secret to read on the train, so I thumbed through a battered paperback. Jasmine pecked away at her laptop. How that was somehow less secret, I don't know. But then, that year, spies were always leaving laptops and secrets on trains – maybe it was standard practice for the Brits?

At the end of the line, it was dark and raining. Jasmine had the keys to an old jeep parked outside the station. We climbed in, and Jasmine bounced me along the dirt tracks to the Monitoring Station. I'd expected it to be dusty or something, but it was spotless.

'That's Sebastian,' she said. 'We couldn't manage without him.'

He met us, courteous and polite and all smiles. He was wearing a suit, even then.

'Sebastian?' I said, staring at him. He was strikingly handsome. 'I have heard so much about you!' I felt stupid saying that. 'It's... a privilege to meet you,' I gushed. Jeez, button it.

'Pleased to meet you,' he said politely and went to put the kettle on.

Jasmine gave me the tour. The hangar was the most exciting bit, naturally. Even now I can't quite believe it... but no.

Then she checked her watch, frowned slightly and announced 'Well, it's all yours now. Any questions, you've got my email and my direct line. It's been so good to get you on board. Don't be a stranger.' Then Sebastian drove her back to the station.

I was left alone in the building. Very excited. Scared witless.

That was the only time I'd ever seen Jasmine. I couldn't even remember what she looked like really. Doll-like, porcelain pale. But there was nothing fragile about her.

Back to that morning, and the inevitable email from Jasmine. At first it seemed no worse than the others, but it was. It was the start of something dreadful.

Hey,

Thanks for the report! Looks great at first glance. 99% there for me first time, so hooray!

There's a few tiny things that just aren't working

for me, though, sorry. Maybe I'm just being slow, but there appears to be no progress on the issues we discussed last time. Should we not try and get them dealt with in the next work cycle? I've had a brief look in the shared folder, but there doesn't seem to be any info there. Am I looking in the wrong place?!? If you could perhaps ping over some data asap on those two topics that are outstanding, then I know that everyone here would be really thrilled.

Hope that's not bombarding you! Let me know if it's getting too much for you, won't you?'

xx Jas x

I stared at the email. Then at two buff folders on my desk. I kept a lot of stuff as hard copy only. After a few early incidents, I knew better than to leave files lying around on the server. Jasmine had a habit of seizing on raw data and twisting it to suit her purposes. That's why I liked those decades-old computers that lined the corridor. They did their job marvellously and just couldn't be linked up to a network. They wouldn't understand what the internet was. They just did their job and issued their reports, burning the information onto ancient sheetfold paper with a reassuring rasp.

I stared again at the two cardboard folders. 'Mind control', said one. 'Aggression', said the other.

I stood up. Jasmine could wait. I was going to the hangar.

I made it as far as the corridor. Sebastian was collecting printouts, folding them neatly and immaculately tearing off the serrated edges. He would do this for most of the morning, then go and spend an hour checking on the flowers that grew around the village.

Tom slouched into the corridor and stood at my elbow, humming and harring, hovering like a fart in a bath. He clearly wanted to say something. I folded away the printout and looked at him.

'Seriously, boss,' he said. 'Can I have a word?' He'd pocketed his phone. Clearly he was giving me his undivided attention.

I nodded. Sometimes you have to accept fate. Fate did not want me to go to the hangar today.

'What is it?' I tried to be businesslike.

'Right,' he began, stumbling a little. 'That family that have turned up in the village?'

'The Williamses?' I nodded. 'Has there been any progress?'

'Progress!' He was angry. 'Tony Brown bloody attacked one of them.'

'What? The policeman?'

'Sexually...' Tom paused. 'Er... Like a sex-starved rabbit.'

I felt a strange, chilly sensation. 'Jeez,' I said.

'The kids picked up on it somehow and stopped it. But it was a close call.'

'Oh my,' I said. 'That's dreadful.'

'I had Megan Harries round demanding something was done,' Tom thundered. He raised an eyebrow. 'It's a real problem, isn't it, boss?'

'The Williamses,' I groaned. 'And that's why we introduced the policy of managed isolation.' I drummed my fingers on a computer casing turned grey with age. 'Rawbone has been gradually closed off from the outside world. I knew that having strangers appear would interfere with the data set.'

'Data set?' Tom was shouting. 'They're people!

The poor woman was bloody traumatised. She was nearly raped.'

Oh my gosh. 'Yeah.' I held up a hand. 'Yeah,' I repeated. 'Is she OK?'

'Kind of,' said Tom. 'I dragged Josh round there last night so I could check on her. Hence the hangover.'

'And the baby?' I felt a knot of tension in my stomach.

'Oh, the child is fine as well. It could have been a lot worse.'

Sebastian spoke up. 'The Scions stopped it going too far.' He looked up from reloading a printer. 'They have followed your standing protocols. A further incident was prevented last night.'

'A further incident?' Tom was alarmed.

Sebastian flicked through a printout, 'The husband went round to the policeman's house.'

'Oh my god,' Tom growled. 'But... when I left them...'

Sebastian passed me the printout. 'The incident was contained... without further harm,' he said.

'By who?' asked Tom.

I leafed through the sheets of green-and-white striped paper. 'Jenny.'

'Hmm,' said Tom.

I knew what he meant. There was something atypical about that girl. Ah well. She was growing up.

'Right then,' I said, sensing any plans I'd had for the day slipping away. 'Tom, can you make sure the Williamses are watched like a hawk? We want them to be OK.'

'Yay,' said Tom, clapping his hands together like

a flamenco dancer. 'More boozing it is.'

'And Sebastian, can you bring me any relevant information on these incidents? Sounds like an interesting near miss. I can actually work all this up into a report for Jasmine the Terrible. We have a perfect set of data here on their containment of aggressive action. That should keep her off our backs for months.'

'Really?' said Tom, his mouth twisted with slight distaste. I knew how bad it sounded. But it could be a lot worse.

'I hope so.' I felt weary, so weary. 'I really hope so.'

Gwen

The dreams got odder. Like I was falling into a strange world where everything was broken. Where the streets of Cardiff were almost empty. First there'd been the strange shadow that had spread over the land, wiping out whoever it touched. Then, not even a year later, one of the Welsh nuclear power stations had blown up. No one had been there to stop it. That had taken out a lot more people.

Those that were left lived out strange lives that got even stranger when something dreadful happened to the Large Hadron Collider in Switzerland. While back in Cardiff reports spread of terrible things occurring – of cannibal cults marching towards the city, of fearsome beasts emerging from the sewers to hunt down the survivors.

Frankly, it was a bit of a mercy when those aliens turned up offering to take our children away. We wanted them to have a better life somewhere else.

Because this planet was finished. Without Torchwood.

I woke up in a lot of pain. OK, a true fact about being an Earth Mother is that it's bloody painful. Gaia – if it's not agony, you're doing it wrong. Breastfeeding is one of those things. I mean, clearly, boys, if you're reading this, you've crossed your legs and your testicles have crawled back inside your pelvis, but breasts are not just jolly fun bags. They have a purpose.

It is to make my life hell.

I used to have an alarm clock. I don't bother any more. When my breasts are full, I wake up. It's not that 'Ooh, quite fancy a pee' thing you get in the middle of the night. No. It's a John-Hurt-In-*Alien* sensation. Good morning world, my boobs are exploding.

I staggered into the living room, a breast pad stuck to my cheek (one always gets there in the middle of the night, dunno how, but I hope Rhys likes his wife smelling a tiny bit like a cheese slice). In the old days, before AD (Anwen Domini), I often used to find Rhys asleep on the sofa, half a bottle of warm beer still held in his hands. Now he's clutching a baby bottle.

Anwen, of course, was in full-on angelic mode, just starting to stir. I picked her up, plugged her in to feed. Her eyes fixed on mine for an instant, then rolled up into her head. She looked truly, blissfully happy.

Once she was back in her cot, I popped the kettle on. Sod what the paper says this week, I'd have coffee. I'd gotten used to having instant again. Shame. I missed proper coffee. More, I missed those days when someone made it for me. No matter how hung over, tired, or attacked by monsters, there'd always be a lovely cup waiting for me. Odd what you take for granted.

I stood there. Life was all back to normal. I had managed not to think about bloody Tony Brown. About the weird kids in the village. It's one of the advantages of your brain turning to post-baby mush.

Some days I can't even really remember my own name.

On cue, Rhys woke up as the kettle boiled and I handed him a mug. He was about to ask me to put some toast on, but I already had. For I am woman, and multitasking is my superpower. It also took my mind off how sore my nipples were, but let's not go there. They say geranium leaves are brilliant for it, but you tell me where I'm supposed to get a geranium leaf in a caravan park in North Wales and I will give you a shiny silver dollar.

Rhys looked a bit rumpled. 'You OK?' I asked him.

'How about you?' he countered.

I just nodded.

He nodded back, a bit shifty and buttered his toast. I'd find out later.

There was a knock at the door, and I opened it instinctively. Foolish, rookie error – forgetting the danger in the village, the men hunting me. I was just too stupidly tired. I wasn't even thinking about the infant clasped to my breast. Standing there was a girl, holding out a newspaper. Early teenage years, but really neatly turned out. Dark hair in no need of straighteners, school uniform worn like no one ever wears school uniform, skin perfect in the way that no 15-year-old has. Right, one of the Scions. I'd met her yesterday, at Mrs Harries's house.

'Jenny?' said Rhys.

I arched an eyebrow. I was not sure how I felt about my husband being on chatty terms with attractive young girls.

Jenny stood waiting on the step, her smile pleasant, and expectant. 'Good morning, Mr Williams. Good morning, Mrs Williams. And how are you today?'

She was making eye contact. No teenage girl makes eye contact. How can these creatures ever have hoped to pass for human?

'Jenny Meredith, isn't it?' I said brightly.

Jenny nodded. 'My mother sent me from the shop to ask if there was anything you would like fetching and also to give you this.' She held out the newspaper. It was open at page 5, with a headline circled in highlighter. I could just read '-stfeeding risk'. Great.

'Come on in, have a cup of coffee.'

Jenny came in, her eyes processing the inside of the caravan critically. It reminded me of whenever Rhys's mother used to visit our old flat. No matter where we cleaned, there'd always be a spot that we'd missed. Jenny's eyes settled on Anwen, fascinated. She politely sipped at a cup of coffee.

'How are you this morning, Mr Williams?' she asked.

'Fine, thanks,' murmured Rhys, his face changing gear to there's-something-I-should-have-told-you-Gwen-but-maybe-I'll-get-away-with-it. Oh, Rhys, love. You will never get away with it.

'I am pleased that you are well,' said Jenny.

'And why wouldn't he be?' I asked pointedly, watching Rhys shrink a little.

Jenny considered the question for a moment. 'Last night Mr Williams attacked our policeman.'

'Oh, he did, did he?' I loved the big, stupid, wonderful fool.

'Yes, I was worried that he would be hurt.'

'Right,' I said, and winked at Rhys. We would deal with this later. Lordy, there was loads to deal with later and not even a spaceship crashing out of the sky.

'Can I hold your baby?' Jenny asked suddenly. 'I have never touched one. It would be interesting.'

Hmm, love, a couple of points there. Mostly, don't act like you might dissect my child.

But I handed Anwen over. My baby girl was wearing that scrunched-up expression that boded really badly for anyone in a three-metre radius. Jenny was welcome to her.

To start with, it was a bit touch and go.

'I am sorry.' Jenny's tone was puzzled. 'I am getting the centre of gravity wrong. Your child is also heavier than she looks.' She paused. 'Tell me, what is her mean atomic weight?'

Even Rhys pulled a face at that, especially as Jenny seemed about to drop Anwen, but we managed a mid-air course correction between us, and, truth to tell, Anwen settled down happily in Jenny's arms. Babies are like cats. No matter how much love and attention you lavish on them, they make a show of being happiest with strangers.

'How old is this?' asked Jenny.

'She's ten weeks,' I said. Rhys, I noticed, had gone to put some more toast on. If he was hoping for distance, he'd best wait till we'd moved somewhere a tiny bit bigger than a large cupboard.

Jenny nodded, interested.

'And how old are you?' I asked.

'Twenty,' said Jenny. I heard Rhys pause, mid-butter scrape.

'Wow,' I said.

Jenny looked down at herself, with a curious air of 'What? This old thing?' She shrugged. 'This is how

I was born. I have always looked like this. I wonder if I always will.'

'Don't you know?'

'No. That is why I said I wondered.'

'Do you...' I paused.

Rhys took over, gently. 'Do you know what you are, Jenny?'

'I am a girl.'

'No... but... the children of the village. You must know... that you're not normal.'

Jenny again paused. If she was a computer she'd have been displaying a gently spinning egg timer. 'But we are normal. Your child is not. It is a different species. It is ageing rapidly. I am not. I am ageing at a much slower rate.'

'Where do you come from?' Rhys asked.

Jenny smiled, the kind of smile you get at the building society when there's been a tiny issue with your account. 'The stork brought us. Or we were found under a gooseberry bush. It is not known.'

'But surely you know that...?'

'Yes,' sighed Jenny. 'That sometimes when a Mummy Bee and a Daddy Bee like each other very much they do a little Baby Dance.' She shook her head. 'But that is not how I was made.' She suddenly looked crestfallen. 'Are there others like us in the world, do you think?'

'No,' I said. 'I don't think so. I think you're very special, Jenny.'

'Special?' echoed Jenny, pleased. 'I like that.'

'What... Tell us about you,' urged Rhys. 'For instance, last night... Jenny... well, she's very strong.'

'I am no stronger than the others, but you grown-ups – your bodies and your minds are weaker than ours.'

'Our minds?' I gasped. Suddenly really worried. Rhys looked the same.

Jenny glanced between us. Like she could read our thoughts. Could she? I felt cold. I felt horribly afraid. This thing... holding my daughter.

Jenny blinked, as though pained. 'Would you like Anwen back?' she offered. Her tone was suddenly that of a real child, trying to share a toy it didn't really want to give up.

'No,' I said quickly. 'It's just... you have to understand, there is something remarkable about you. What do you mean about our minds being weak?'

'Oh...' Jenny was casual. 'It is so hard to explain. Your minds are like jelly. It is really easy to push them and make them wobble. It is fun. But we do not. We are told not to.'

'Who tells you not to?' Rhys asked. Good point.

Jenny shrugged. 'I cannot explain.'

'But why are you here?' I asked.

'Because Rawbone is a sad place. We are trying to make the people here happier.'

'How's that working out for you, then?' asked Rhys dourly.

For an instant, Jenny shot him such a look. Then, like a summer cloud, it passed, and she was all radiant bafflement. 'We do the best we can.'

'But who brought you here in the first place?' I asked. 'I mean, Jenny, you must have some idea of that?'

She shook her head, and her gloriously straight hair barely moved. 'No. I am still a child. I do not believe that a child understands the meaning of life.'

I was about to say that she had a massive whiff of bullshit about her, when she paused, sniffed and wrinkled her nose. 'This baby, it is now wrong,' she said.

'Oh,' I said. 'Anwen just needs changing, that's all.'

'Into what?' Jenny looked puzzled.

'She needs a new nappy,' I explained.

'Oh.' Jenny smiled widely. 'What is that? Is it fun? Can I try?'

'By all means.' I smiled. 'Jenny, do you know what pebble-dashing means?'

She shook her head.

'Then this will be fun.'

Rhys

I watched Jenny holding our baby.

We kind of skipped antenatal classes, due to being hunted by the world's secret police, but one of the things I was dying to have a go on was a fake baby. You know the things I mean? They're dolls, they weigh about the same, they make a lot of noise and are constantly demanding. But they're not actually real.

Suddenly, that's what Jenny reminded me of. A kid that had been made in a factory. But by who, and why?

Despite my reservations, she was bloody good with the baby, that was for certain. I realised that Jenny was great at picking up and reflecting body language. Anwen frowned, so Jenny would frown. Which would make Anwen smile. So Jenny would smile. The baby even stopped squirming and hung in her arms, as floppy as an old T-shirt

Suddenly, Gwen and I had nothing to do. We were just stood there at the side of the kitchen-dinette.

'Don't you have somewhere to be?'

Jenny shrugged. 'Only school.' She paused. 'But today I am *mitching off*.' She used slang like a BBC newsreader. I wondered if I could get her to say 'cowing lush'.

Gwen took a step closer and sank down, staring at Jenny's eye level. She was in Nancy Drew mode.

'School, right?'

'Yes.'

'Do you learn stuff?'

'Heaps.' Jenny considered. 'I think I know a lot of it already. But sometimes it is nice for us all to learn together.'

'And what do you learn?'

'Stuff.' Jenny's eyes, just for a second slid sideways and then back. Evasive. Cunning. Sly.

'What kind of stuff?' Gwen hadn't missed a thing.

'We are not supposed to say,' Jenny admitted. She held up Anwen. 'I believe she is hungry. Shall I feed her?' She started to unbutton her school shirt.

'No, it's OK.' Gwen was very quick. 'I'll take care of it.'

Jenny refused lunch, which was a shame, as I'd managed something approaching a proper meal, even if it was from tins. At the stroke of two o'clock, she stood up.

'I will go now, if that is all right,' she said. She handed Anwen over to me. I held the baby up above my head and dangled her, then swept her to my shoulder, making embarrassing 'Who's Daddy's favourite girl?' noises.

Jenny watched impassively. 'I must go to games.'

'Oh, right,' said Gwen.

'I have enjoyed playing with your child, however.'

'Anwen,' I put in.

'Yes,' agreed Jenny. 'Perhaps I can do so again? Anwen is small and warm.'

'And smells,' I said.

'Yes. Would you like me to change her again

before I go?'

'Nah,' I said. 'It's what dads are for.'

'I see.' Jenny nodded. 'I had wondered what part they played after the conception.' She smiled. 'I must go. Have a good afternoon.' She turned around and left.

We watched her walk out of the caravan park, her perfect hair and neatly ironed school uniform all utterly in place.

'Crikey,' I said.

'Yeah,' said Gwen.

'So,' I muttered, 'we've got one of the Children of the Corn as a babysitter.'

'All I heard,' Gwen pushed her hair away from her face, 'was the word "babysitter".'

'Yeah,' I agreed dreamily.

We worked out what to do next. Then we drew up a list. We drew up a lot of lists in those days. Normally while the bottle steriliser was cooking up its sweet little hospital-whiffing stew of Milton fluid.

'So, we find out what the Scions really are, investigate the Weather Monitoring Station, find out where these kids go to school. Anything else?' Gwen asked. She was holding a biro quite seriously, even though she'd scribbled the list on the back of a takeaway menu.

'Pop into the village shop for bog roll,' I said.

'Yes,' agreed Gwen. 'That goes straight to the top of the list.'

Eloise

Hey Eloise!

Thanks so much for this. Great stuff. Really feel we've moved on. We are making progress, so yay!

Small thing. Just wondering if you have any more data about this family who have moved into Rawbone you can cycle downstream? I've checked the databases on the shared folder, and there's nothing in there, unless I am being stupid and missing it. I'd really appreciate it if you could keep the shared folder up to date! These systems aren't just for my benefit, but for the entire project! So, sorry, but can you update them if you've got a moment to spare? Everyone here is very keen to know what's going on with this family. Pictures too, if you've got a chance to take them, that would be fab. Would really appreciate the effort.

Main thing, obviously, is that the info about how the Scions are reacting to the outside influence is BLOODY FASCINATING. Great data, really. Risky stuff, but paying off. Lot of thought going on here as to how we can utilise it – maybe bring in more parents with children, see how that provokes things? Shake it up and see what falls out! We'll have more thoughts for you on that soon.

Obv, keen to hear any ideas you've got as to how you can minimise the effect this is having on the adult population. That would be great. Love to see some action on that asap, naturally. We don't want a

bloodbath on our hands! :)
   Let's really step it up and mix it up, yeah?
   x Jas x

I gazed at the screen. Tom was reading it over my shoulder. I hadn't even heard him come in.

'Oh eM Gee,' he said. 'She's really talking about bringing more children into Rawbone?'

'Uh-huh.' My voice was little more than a whisper.

'But how?' He was really angry. Really angry with me. Like this was my fault.

'I'm fairly sure it's impossible, isn't it?' I protested.

Tom shrugged. 'She'll probably resettle a few asylum seekers. They've always got lots of children. Children and nasty jumpers.'

'Jeez,' I groaned.

'What the hell are we going to do?' Tom muttered.

I stood up, tugging down my cardigan. 'Let's run away. We could open up a tea shop somewhere.'

Tom finally smiled, slightly. 'We'd have to take Sebastian with us.'

'True,' I agreed.

We wandered out into the corridor. Sebastian was there, as ever, reloading the paper into the sheet feeder. I loved that ancient printer. Noisy but reliable. No one knew where Sebastian got the supplies for it – there was probably a bunker somewhere full of that lovely green and white lined paper with perforated holes down the sides. Just the smell of it took me back to my childhood, to the Computer Room at high school, to lessons in Chemistry and Biology, to standing over a Bunsen burner with a tiny slice of liver bubbling away in a test tube.

Confession – my first ever science lesson, I was a total klutz. True fact. I heated up a test tube over a Bunsen. No one had told me anything about glass conducting heat. Why should I know that? I know it's common sense, but I'm not a common-sense gal. So I didn't use the metal tongs, I just waved the test tube over the flame with my hands. Cost me a couple of blistered fingertips, but taught me some really useful stuff.

Like don't conduct a scientific experiment before you know all of the facts.

Sebastian stood impassively watching a dot matrix printer scream importantly away. He saw my expression. 'Is it bad news?'

I nodded, telling him what Jasmine was planning.

'What do you think?' I asked him. I was interested to know. He knew more about the children than anyone.

There was a pause. He considered the question, politely and seriously. He neatly folded up the printouts, handing them over to me.

'It sounds like a bad idea,' he announced eventually. His voice was even. His face placid. But I could tell he was still thinking.

'What do you think will happen?'

'I do not like to speculate,' Sebastian admitted. 'But based on the evidence, the hosts will reject the Scions.'

'Yeah,' I said. 'And how will the Scions take it?'

'Bloody, bloody badly.' This was Tom, storming past like an angry little firecracker. 'Ciggie break.

Don't start a war while I'm gone, will you?'

He kind of had a point. I stood there, shaking slightly.

You know how sometimes you're so stressed, you just don't know what to do next? And then the longer you stand there, the gears in your brainbox grinding unhappily away, the worse it gets? This was one of those days. One of those terrible, I am going to do nothing, all-over-the-place days.

Sebastian made me a cup-a-soup and I gave myself the luxury of going into the hangar. I needed to see something beautiful.

Gwen

Getting the pram there was bloody murder. Let me make this absolutely clear – prams nowadays may have chunky wheels and look like you could go mountain-biking with one, but anything approaching an uphill slope on a gravel path and they start to behave like they're being pushed through porridge.

But I made it to the Weather Monitoring Station eventually. The afternoon drizzle was biting at my face. I'd pulled the special baby cagoule-canopy over the front of the pram, so Anwen looked like she was in some kind of slow-moving moon rover, being shoved along by a damp, fat bag lady.

The Weather Monitoring Station looked pretty much how you'd expect it to look. A collection of fairly unglamorous leftovers from the Second World War. The armed forces had requisitioned a fair chunk of North Wales, picking out the really, really beautifully unspoilt bits, then built corrugated-iron and concrete sheds on them. This one even had a runway, crazy-paved with moss and those weird stink thistle flowers were everywhere. The whole base was surrounded by quite a nice-looking chain fence. Two sets. Modern. Razor wire. Around a Weather Monitoring Station. Because if there's one thing the weather needs, it's carefully protecting.

I found Tom standing on the other side of the chain fence, fiddling with his phone and smoking away. He boggled guiltily at me and looked like he was going to bolt back indoors.

I waved. 'Morning! Just taking the little one for a walk!'

'Here?' He was alarmed. 'Really?'

'Don't suppose there's any chance of a tour, is there?'

He shook his head. 'You must be joking.'

'I'm breastfeeding, I don't have time for jokes.'

We stood there. Separated by the chain fence. Like we were in one of those war films. 'I feel I should be pushing food through the fence to you,' I said. 'But I don't have anything.'

'Not even rusks?' he asked. 'I bloody love those.'

'No. She's too young.'

'Pity,' he sighed. 'I might have been persuaded.'

'Liar.'

He shrugged. 'Just trying to make you feel bad.'

He flicked his cigarette away. It spiralled through the air and landed on the runway with a *pfffst*.

'So,' I asked, 'how's the weather?'

Tom held out a hand. 'Damp,' he said. He reached into his windcheater, pulling out his packet of cigarettes. 'Want one?' he asked.

'Nah.' I sighed. 'Even if I did, I'm probably not allowed one for another twenty years or so.'

'Is it OK me smoking?'

'In the open air, within ten feet of a baby?' I smiled. 'Mumsnet will hunt you down.'

He lit up and grinned at me. 'Drives Josh mad. Officially, I gave up six months ago. Yet strangely, whenever I get home from work, I stink of it. Pretty sure he's on to me. But I just tell him that Eloise smokes like a chimney.'

'Eloise?'

For a second he blinked. He'd made a small error. 'Yeah. You must have seen her cruising around in the world's oldest jeep. She's my boss.' He leaned forward confidentially, his nose touching the chain-link fence. 'She is an American.'

'Here?' I boggled.

'I know. She's about 300 miles away from a mochachino or Ashtanga yoga. God knows how she copes.'

'So,' I asked, 'what's she doing here?'

He waved the cigarette at me in a naughty-naughty way. 'We have really interesting weather.'

'So interesting she's come halfway round the world?'

'Oh yes,' Tom's voice was dry. 'Along with a suitcase full of chunky knits and disapproval. She is an absolute delight.'

'I'll look her up.'

'Do,' said Tom.

We were silent for a bit. Not quite a comfortable silence. More a 'whose turn is it?' silence. I pointed to the flowers littering the runway. 'What are those things?'

Tom shrugged too casually. 'Weeds?'

'Rhys says the villagers call them stink thistles.'

'Good name,' Tom said.

'They're all over the village. I've never seen them anywhere else.'

'Ah.' Tom wasn't being drawn. 'Funny that.'

He finished the cigarette in one last, long exhale, the smoke meeting the drizzle in a big cloud like a snow globe. *Pfffst*. He jammed his hands in his pockets and looked at me.

'How are you?' he asked, his tone completely different. Serious. Worried.

'I've felt better,' I admitted.

'I'm still so sorry about the whole thing.' He paused, shiftily. 'If you want my advice...'

I smiled. 'Go on.'

'Leave.'

'Excuse me?'

'Please leave. Rawbone isn't a place to bring up a kid.'

I shook my head and smiled at him. 'You do know I'm staying put, don't you?'

'Yeah,' Tom admitted glumly.

We stood there.

'Go on,' I said, 'Let me in. Just for a quick look round.'

'Nice try.' He turned to go. 'Gwen?'

'Yes?'

'What did you do? Before you came here? Were you really a policewoman?'

'Something like that,' I admitted. 'But I'm on maternity leave now.'

'Funny place to pick,' said Tom, and walked back inside the building, saying goodbye with a cheery wave.

Rhys

Perhaps I should have gone shopping after I'd found the school. As it was I felt a bit stupid creeping around the village with two bags of groceries.

Jenny's mum had been serving, and had loaded me down with lots of stuff. I noticed that there was now a whole shelf of nappies, antiseptic wipes, and jars of baby food proudly on display. Mrs Meredith had seemed crestfallen when I'd just bought baked beans and some toilet paper, so I'd ended up hunting through the nappies.

'Right then,' I muttered, aware that Mrs Meredith was watching me like an excited pigeon. 'What size are these?'

'Baby size,' said Mrs Meredith, a trace of uncertainty in her tone. 'Why, what do you mean?'

'Well…' I held up a packet. 'There are several sets of sizes – for a start there's three sizes of Newborn and then there's Baby Dry, but they kind of overlap. You don't want to get that one wrong. What we really want is a size 3 in the Baby Dry, I reckon, but we've kind of been squeezing her into a Newborn size 2.'

I'd been waiting so long to get this stuff off my chest. I tried for a knowing chuckle.

'Well, she's not turned purple yet! Truth be known, it's how we'll tell the difference between size 4 and size 4+ that's really worrying me. Then there's the fits – do you go for active or snuggle? Can't quite see which one this is. Can you?'

Mrs Meredith squinted and then sagged. 'I just ordered in nappies.' Her voice was miserable.

'Ah, not to worry,' I said quickly, and grabbed a pack of 84 of the things, hoping they wouldn't leak and bring down the wrath of Gwen on me. She always knows the right size of nappy to buy. Instinct.

'Is that all?' asked Mrs Meredith.

I picked up a tin of banana-and-custard baby food which, actually, I quite fancied the look of. I decided to take the opportunity to sniff out some intelligence. 'So,' I asked, super casual, 'there's a school in town?'

'Oh yes, dear,' she said. 'In the old village hall. We used to send the kids down to town, but nowadays that's quite enough...' She dried up, as though she'd said something wrong. Yet another half-truth.

She then hurriedly asked me a lot of stuff about Anwen, how she was doing, how she was sleeping, whether she was still being breastfed, how she took to the bottle and whether we put her down on her side or her back. She'd clearly been devouring the Daily Hate again, as she was as confused as me about the merits of lying her on her back. I sometimes wonder if that paper believes that the women of Britain are on the tipping point of revolution and the only way to prevent this is by keeping them worried about accidentally killing their children, opening the floodgates to foreigners or dropping dead from cancer.

Anyway, we were setting in for quite a good natter when I remembered the job at hand. Mrs Meredith gave me some fairly sketchy directions to the village hall, something like 'walk past the house that used to belong to the Richardsons – oh, of course, you've never met them, lovely couple, but they've retired now, then past the barns, along the old town road, past a clump of stink thistles, and within a couple of minutes you'll be there, can't miss it. Nice old building, it is, but it does get ever so draughty. They say the roof needs redoing but I've no idea how we'll ever afford to do that. You know how it is...'

I agreed that I did know how it was, thanked her, and left on manoeuvres.

There I stood, crouched low behind a notice board, looking at the village hall. It was the solidest building in Rawbone. If there were a nuclear blast, this would be where the cockroaches would hang out.

I slipped through the gate, crept down the path and towards the window. It was at this point that I realised I should have done the shopping later. There's a reason you never see James Bond perched on a hotel balcony with a bag-for-life containing a pint of semi-skimmed, that week's *Inside Soap*, and 20 Bensons. Information: it is almost impossible to stealthily put down a carrier that's got tins of beans in it. It sounded like a metal cat falling off the roof. Not even a ninja could carry it off.

I peered through the window. At a semicircle of teenagers. The children of Rawbone. Standing there at the front was Mrs Harries. She was scribbling on a whiteboard. The children were watching. I don't know what I'd been expecting, really.

This is a stupid thing to realise when you're standing on tiptoe, gripping on to a windowsill with your fingernails and pressed up against a window, trying to read the writing on a distant whiteboard. If I was looking for a heading labelled 'Invasion Plan' then I was in for a disappointment. They seemed to be learning French.

I listened in to the lesson for a bit. There was something wrong about it. I was sure of that. They were all very good. Mrs Harries would start to speak and they would repeat it. *Écoutez et répétez!* That was it!

The children continued their French lesson

'*Il y a un homme à la fenêtre!*'

There was something... not quite right...

'*Qui est l'homme qui est à la fenêtre?*'

That was it! They weren't waiting for a response. They were speaking at the same time as Mrs Harries. That was impossible, surely...

'*L'homme qui nous espionne, il s'appelle Rhys Williams.*'

What?

The children of Rawbone all turned to me and smiled. In unison. Mrs Harries waved. They all waved too.

Merde, I thought.

Mrs Harries beckoned me in. Thoroughly rumbled, and feeling like I'd just been caught carving a weeping willy on my desk, I slunk through the door.

'*Bonjour, Monsieur Rhys!*' chorused the children of Rawbone, grinning.

'*Bonjour,*' I said weakly.

Mrs Harries started speaking.

'So what do you—' the children chorused simultaneously.

Mrs Harries held up a finger and shushed them. They shushed her back and then giggled. 'Sorry,' she said. 'It's how they learn. It's brilliant, isn't it?'

'Uhhhh...' I began, but she cautioned me.

'Think carefully before you judge us. After all, we're not the ones fogging up windows staring at teenagers. We'd so hate for you to end up on a list.' She wagged a friendly finger and then rested against the table, her hands jammed in her coat pockets. She looked amused and at ease. I noticed that her body language was, just slightly, echoed by the Scions.

'So... ah...' I mumbled.

'Tell you what, Mr Williams... the children will answer any questions you have for them. If you ask it...' She paused and smiled. 'If you ask it in French.'

'What's French for "bollocks"?' I said.

The children laughed. It was odd. All of them – in the room together, ever so neat and identical and orderly and yet... just slightly... For instance, I could tell the ones who were Mrs Harries's children. Peter and Paul – their hair had a slight curl to it. There was an almost untidiness to them that you couldn't quite put a finger on, but all the same, you thought that another pass with the iron wouldn't go amiss. And yet, all of them together, oddly identical. Black hair, clear blue eyes. Like if the Hitler Youth had gone to the Eisteddfod.

Suddenly aware I was the centre of attention, I shifted nervously. The children of Rawbone shifted. One fiddled with a pen. Another whistled. A ripple of unease went through the room.

'Right then... I mean, *Maintenant*. Er, *oui*?'

'*Oui.*'

'*Pourquoi est tu...* no, sorry – *Pourquoi êtes-vous là?*'

'*Ici,*' put in Mrs Harries helpfully.

'*Je ne sais pas,*' chorused the children of Rawbone.

Blankly.

'*Vraiment?*' I asked them.

'*Non, nous n'avons pas reçu des instructions.*'

'*Quoi?*'

'*Les instructions. Nous attendons.*'

'Sorry – what? I mean…? Just tell me, OK… Er… *Dites-moi! Dites-moi!*'

'*Nous ne comprenons pas. Nous ne comprenons pas.*' The children repeated.

'But surely… Sorry, hang on. *Mais, vraiment, vous doits…*'

A chair scraped back. One of the kids, Peter, stood there. Staring at me. 'We don't know,' he said.

The other chairs were pushed back, toppling over, one after the other. The children stood. Suddenly angry. Very angry. 'We don't know,' they cried. Not in unison. Not together. Not chanting. Just a babble. A confused, furious babble. Aimed at me.

Oh my god.

It was like trying to stand up in icy, horizontal rain. A blast that shook me. The sheer cold – at first it was like a wall in front of my eyes, then I felt it wrap around me like a wet towel… cold and sharp… the worst ice cream headache ever. Then it squeezed.

Behind me, Mrs Harries moaned and fell to the floor. 'Children! Stop it,' she cried out.

'What are you doing?' I shouted. 'Please! What are you doing?'

The shouting cacophony continued. I tried to shut my eyes, but I was blind – all I could see were colours dancing and jiggling and then I started to feel my feet giving way.

Each word stabbed at my head.

'We! Don't! Know! Leave! Us! Alone!'

I was on the floor. I knew that. My senses jumping around. The floor smelt just like every old wooden floor – polish and plimsolls.

'Leave! Us! Alone!'

I slept.

Gwen

I pushed Anwen back through the village. It seemed cold and empty, even for Rawbone. I could hear Anwen stirring and murmuring. Like she was having a bad dream. After a few steps... oh, you know how when you're walking home alone late at night, and you suddenly become convinced that you're being followed? That there is something behind you, just out of the corner of your eye? Something that means you harm? It was that feeling. The rain had pooled into a mist, a mist that pressed in on the streets, turning the houses into ghosts.

I was utterly alone. The feelings washed over me. Emotions, wave after wave of them – of fear, of anger, of loneliness and confusion and despair. I could hear Anwen crying and I lifted her out of her pram. 'Oh, baby,' I said, hugging her close. 'You feel it too, don't you? Come on, little miss, it'll be OK.' Her crying got louder and louder. Echoing off the wet stone walls.

A curtain twitched distantly.

It was Sasha. She stood there in her front room, looking at me holding my baby. She didn't offer to help, or even acknowledge me. She just watched. Like she was sheltering from the storm.

I didn't care. I left the pram, grabbed Anwen, and ran to Sasha's door, hammering on it. She'd bloody let me in.

*

I sat in her living room. It was plain but comfortable. Like she'd been to a sale at Furniture World a few years ago. A throw stretched over a fuzzy peach sofa. Dusty candles sat on coffee tables next to teddy bears. There were old dried flowers and a comfy rug that needed hoovering.

I held Anwen to me until she stopped crying. Somehow, holding her near made me feel better.

Sasha brought out two cups of tea. Her mug had a penguin, mine had a panda. The tea was weak and grey. She settled down opposite me. Angry.

'What was that?' I asked. 'What was going on outside?'

'Happens,' she shrugs. 'Sometimes. Folks know to stay clear of it.'

'That wasn't rain or mist. That was...' I tried to explain. But I just couldn't. My thoughts were little mice being stood on. Another mystery in Rawbone that no one spoke about.

'Yeah. Whatever.' Sasha's shrug was heavy, guarded. 'We know better than to be out in it. You can feel it coming so you get out of the way. When you've been here long enough, you'll know.' She flicked through a magazine, not meeting my eye.

'But what causes it? Is it the children?' I asked.

She didn't look up from the magazine. 'We don't ask. We don't talk about it. If you're planning on staying, you won't either.'

I smiled at her. 'Well, perhaps someone should find out.'

'I think you've got enough on your plate. With the baby and all,' she said, sourly.

'The problem—' I countered, and then stopped. Don't be rude, Gwen Cooper, don't be bloody rude.

No, sod it. 'The problem with this place is that no one asks. There's so much wrong, but you just accept what's happening. This village has suffered a terrible tragedy – it's not just that you've got no kids. It's that you've stopped asking why. It's that you've got these... creatures. And you don't even know what they are.'

'No.' Sasha had closed the magazine and was gripping her mug, her hands tight round the capering penguin. 'We don't know. But they're what we've got. They're all we've got. So we get on with it. You wouldn't know. Look at all you have. But you're not just smug about it – you are judging us. Just cos you're fertile doesn't give you the right to act like you're BETTER. You've just got a bloody baby, that's all.'

'What about yours?' I asked. 'You have got a child of your own, yeah?'

'Billy,' she shrugged, dismissively. 'He's... he's fine. He's 15. I'm 24. He's been my kid for three years. And he's always been like that. Not growing up. We don't bother with birthdays. Ever since I opened the door that morning and he was stood there. "Hello mother." Those were his first words.' She scowled. 'When he bloody came in he asked if there was anything he could help with. Any cleaning, or tidying, or if I would like a cup of bloody tea. Didn't even ask if he could come in. Davydd just let him. I didn't want him and there was no getting rid of him.' She stopped and her eyes were fixed on a patch of artex over the fake mantelpiece. She stared at it harder and harder and I realised she was trying not to cry. 'Davydd was fine about it... but then he's always been bloody fine about it. Don't think he even wanted kids that much.

He'd have coped all right, yeah. He just wanted them cos I wanted them. Anything for a quiet life. And he gets a kid that gives him a quiet life. That doesn't play up, or answer back, that does its own washing. That clears up after itself. That never gets ill or stays out late. Billy plays on the Xbox with him. But never beats him at it. Oh, Davydd's never spotted that bit. Stupid boy.' The last bit was said fondly. She tugged at the necklace round her throat. 'He's just relieved. That I've got something a bit like a kid. That'll keep me happy. It's close enough for him. Like when Davydd tried to put up shelves. "Only a bit wonky, soon settle down," he said. But it's a child... a child...' She stopped again. 'What can you know?' she said finally.

Anwen started to cry again. She was glaring at me. I knew what that look meant.

'Listen,' I said, feeling awkward. 'She needs a feed. Can I use your bathroom?'

Sasha picked up the magazine. 'No, no, do it here. *Dim problem.*'

I fed Anwen. Sasha sitting in stony silence, glaring at me. The magazine was held in front of her, but she wasn't reading it. She was just watching me feed my baby. A tear formed, ran down her cheek, and hit the paper with a bang.

'What am I like?' she cried, standing up. She snatched the mugs off the table, emptied them down the sink, ran them quickly under the cold tap then banged them down on the draining board. She stood over the sink, staring out of the window.

Rhys

I dreamed.

'So when do we get to see her?' My mother's voice boomed down the phone.

'Ah…' I said.

'We're ever so excited,' she gushed, clearly not hearing the panic in my voice. 'A granddaughter! We've got her a teddy.' A pause. 'That is, if Gwen approves of teddies.'

My mother has never quite accepted or understood Gwen. I sometimes wonder who my mother would have considered suitable, but it's definitely never quite been Gwen. I'd kind of hoped that would have changed with the wedding, but it didn't. Torchwood got in the way.

Her mood changed just a little with the announcement of the pregnancy, but then, well, Torchwood got in the way again.

And then we went on the run. Or, as I put it, 'Freelance Contracting.'

'And what does that even mean?' My mother sounded so sad on the phone. 'Don't forget your pension. After all, Gwen's not the type to go back to work after having a baby, and you'll have an extra mouth to feed, and it's important to think about these things.'

This was my mother – a woman who cut her pot scrubbers in half to make them last twice as long.

There was no place in her world for Gwen or for Torchwood.

She took the news that we wouldn't be paying a visit with bitter stoicism. 'Ah well, I'm sure Gwen thinks that's for the best.'

I started to argue, but she just steamrollered over me. 'Listen, Rhys, have you got an address? So that we can post on that teddy. That is, if Gwen wants it. I know you're moving around a lot, but it would be nice to think that our grandchild had something of ours with her.'

I explained that we didn't really have an address. I didn't say we were staying at a motor lodge on a traffic island near Tenby.

'Are you sure there isn't an address, love?' My mother pressed on. 'It's just that there were some old friends of hers from work round here the other day looking for her. Quite why they think I could help, I do not know. But they're ever so keen to get in touch with her.'

I imagined them. Sat in the front room while my mum fussed around them with shop-bought cake and the floral-pattern china. They probably wore suits and smiles and sunglasses indoors and were ever so polite.

They were still coming for us. And they wouldn't stop.

I woke up.

'Oh dear,' said Mrs Harries, her voice ever so weak. 'You set them off.'

We were both lying down on the floor of the empty village hall.

'What the bloody hell happened?' It felt like a

terrible, terrible hangover. A sharp nail was being hammered into my skull right between the eyes.

'You'll have taken the brunt of it, my dear,' Mrs Harries looked similarly pained and her hands were shaking. 'They don't get upset... often.' She sat up, rubbing at her head. Blood trickled from a nostril. She fished around in her handbag, chomped down a couple of aspirin and offered me the blister pack. 'No water, I'm afraid, but it's better than bugger all.'

I swallowed the pills and wondered how long it would be before I could feel them doing some good. About twenty minutes wasn't it? Twenty minutes suddenly seemed such a long time.

'Where are they?' I asked.

Mrs Harries's eyes flicked to the door, nervously. 'They always make themselves scarce afterwards. Sheepish.'

'What.... What was it that they did?' I asked, massaging my forehead, which only succeeded in moving the pain around a bit.

'It's...' Her voice was tight and strained. The poor woman was clearly terrified. As she spoke, I felt a chill spread through the room. She wrapped her jacket tightly around her like it was a blanket. 'It was... It's what happens when...'

'Wait. You're saying they can control minds?'

'Not exactly... but they can... Oh, it's tough to say. Really, we know so little about them. But they can influence their parents. It's hard to explain. On a hot summer's day, Mrs Meredith sells out of ice cream very rapidly.'

That was utterly creepy.

'Normally, it's fine. You'll find yourself picking up a few extra things on the supermarket run, doing a special wash for a favourite T-shirt, or watching a TV programme you don't much care for... but that's it.'

There was something oddly human about this. Favourite TV programmes and T-shirts? These kids seemed a bit less unsettling. A bit more like human children. Just with better pester power. Only... only they'd just turned my brain off and then back on again.

'Every now and then... they get locked into... well, a loop. It's your fault this time, I'm afraid.' Mrs Harries ran a finger around the old wooden floor. 'You got angry and scared, they got angry and scared. You were frustrated, and they beamed it right back at you...'

'Couldn't you stop it?'

Mrs Harries shook her head. 'Oh, when they get like that, it's not easy. I was trying, but it's hard to send out calming feelings when you just want to climb up the curtains screaming.'

Good point.

'It's the other reason why I teach the kids. To learn about them. To try... well, I hope, if not to bond with them, at least to understand them better.' She looked tired. 'I don't. They're like real children I guess. You just can't know what they're thinking.'

I patted her on the arm. Now I'd been on the receiving end of what they could do, I realised that it took guts to be in the same room with them. 'They don't age, do they?'

'No,' she said.

'So you're stuck with a village full of eternal teenagers. No wonder they can't control what they're thinking.'

'You're bang on the money there, dear.' Ruefully, Mrs Harries pulled herself to her feet and shook herself down like a wet dog. 'It's so sad. We had no idea… at first we thought they would age. That they would grow up and become more… normal. But they don't change. Not really. They're always on the edge of becoming adults. Well, they do… alter a little. It's like they are growing up, but at ever such a slow rate. We decided not to send them out to a real school… when we saw what they could do with their minds…'

'Right,' I said. 'What do we do now?'

'We go and find them,' Mrs Harries said, and she looked so scared. 'They'll be waiting for us outside.'

She took my arm and we left the village hall. The streets seemed deserted. We found Mrs Harries's children in the playground, Peter and Paul sat placidly on the swings, the only sound the echoing creak of old metal chains swaying back and forth as the children watched us, staring right through us. It was chilling.

'Hello mother,' said the oldest, slipping off the swing. 'Are you feeling better?'

'Yes,' she said, a slight catch in her voice. I felt her grip my arm tightly. 'Yes, I'm much better now.' She smiled at them, ever so brave.

'Good,' said Peter, running up to her. 'I am so glad. I am hungry. What are you going to cook for us?'

Her two children dragged her away home. She turned around to say goodbye to me, and there was a look of utter terror on her face. Then she went quietly on her way.

Gwen

Back at home. Safe and sound. Just sit down. Sit down and chill. Just for a minute.

Best put the kettle on, though. Sort out some laundry. Work out what needs doing. Fold away the dry clothes. Put the recycling to one side. Fish the bottles out of the steriliser. Wipe down the kitchen unit where Rhys has left some crumbs. It never ends.

Then Anwen started crying and needed changing. You don't want to know what happened next, but I had to throw my top on the laundry pile, and try and find a clean one. These days I have more outfit changes than Lady Gaga. Weird how a few months ago the correct answer to 'How much urine is acceptable on a shirt?' was 'None'. Now it's a bit of sliding scale, to be honest.

The kettle had boiled and cooled. I heated it up again, found a teabag. We were out of milk. Which was kind of ironic. Anyway, I finally flopped down in the chair. It had taken twenty minutes. But finally, a moment all to myself.

Guiltily I caught my eyes sliding to the door, praying Rhys wouldn't come home. Just a couple of minutes... that'd be all...

I walked into Sasha's house. She was standing there, arms folded tightly. Simmering with rage.

'There you are, Billy,' she yelled, grabbing me by the ear. 'Where've you bloody been?' She slapped me round the face, twice. Furious and burning with anger.

'Cry!' she screamed. 'Why won't you bloody cry, Billy?'

'Would it make you happy if I did?' I asked.

She hit me again.

'I can cry if you would like,' I said.

The blows rained down, and she cursed at me, saying I wasn't a proper child. That I was fake. That I was useless. That she hated me. That I had ruined her life.

'But Mother,' I said. 'What have I done wrong?' I wanted her to tell me. To list the things that were unacceptable so that I could correct them. That is all I wanted to do.

Instead she just punched me, screaming over and over again that I was filthy. She dragged me upstairs, slapping hard at me. Each blow stung me, and there was no time to recover before the next one landed. I wanted to fight back, but the voice in my head told me not to.

So I stood in the bathroom, smarting. She started to run a bath. She screamed at me. So I took my clothes off slowly.

'Get in!' she yelled, dragging me off my balance.

I stepped into the bath. But it was hot. Too hot. I told her this.

'I don't bloody care,' she snarled, twisting the hot water on full.

'I would like to get out,' I said, my voice simple. The water was very hot. It hurt me. Burnt me.

'You're not getting out!' And she hit me again,

grabbing hold of me, pushing me down under the scalding water...

Gasping, I opened my eyes. It was dark. The sun had set. Someone was standing over me.

Oh my god.

No. OK. It was just Jenny. Standing there. Ever so polite, watching me, arms held in front of her like she was about to pray.

'Jenny!' I shouted. I was startled.

'Good evening, Mrs Williams,' she said. Her tone of voice was even, considered. 'I knocked but you did not answer.'

'So you just came in?'

Jenny shrugged. 'Yes. I wanted to make sure the baby and you were OK.' She said *OK* like it was a foreign word. Like a newsreader saying 50 Cent. 'How is Anwen?'

'She's fine, thanks. We're fine. Shouldn't we be?' A sudden fear. Where was Rhys? I could still feel my heart pounding from the dream.

Jenny shrugged. 'I was just making sure. Babies do require a lot of attention.'

'Tell me about it,' I said, standing up to put the kettle on.

'I was hoping you would tell me all about it. I would like to learn,' offered Jenny. Her clinical gaze considered me. I now knew what it was like to be under a microscope.

'Oh,' I said, trying to be casual. On an impulse, I handed Anwen over. 'Here, hold her. Jenny, you're my Number One Babysitter.'

As she took the baby, Jenny smiled, a big radiant happiness that showed off her lovely teeth. She seemed much more like a real, actual human child. She cupped the baby to her, holding her up above her head and dangling her, then sweeping her to her shoulder. 'You are Jenny's favourite girl,' she said warmly. Anwen cooed delightedly, flashing one of her lazy little smiles before settling back off to a firm sleep. 'She is so warm,' gushed Jenny.

'Yeah,' I forced a smile. I tried to ignore the horrible panic gnawing away at my stomach. That dream. That horrible dream...

Rhys came staggering in, wrapping me in a big hug. 'Hey gorgeous,' he grinned, 'I've had a mad day – those bloody kids are...' He caught sight of Jenny, stopped and stared. 'Are you...' he began, alarmed by something. 'Gwen, is it OK for her to...?'

'Do not worry.' I realised Jenny was talking to me. 'Mr Williams is afraid of us at the moment.'

'Why?' I asked.

Rhys looked stricken. 'I've seen what they can do, Gwen.'

'I see.' Jenny nodded, unfussed. 'You got caught in the storm, didn't you?'

Rhys nodded.

'The storm?' I asked.

'Brain storm, Mrs Harries calls it,' she said. 'Sometimes our thoughts get out of control.' She held a hand out to Rhys. 'I am sorry. It will not have been pleasant.'

'No.' Rhys shook his head. 'It bloody wasn't.'

On an impulse, I spoke up. 'I just had this really odd dream...'

'That will have been us.' To Jenny this was the most normal thing in the world. 'Sometimes we enter people's thoughts. Yours.'

'Why me?' I asked.

'Oh, just because,' she said, airily. She suddenly looked sly. 'You are dreaming a lot, aren't you? Mothers have a high degree of empathy with their newborn children... It's a bond that we could unconsciously intrude on. And you are very tired... the boundary between asleep and awake is so thin for you.'

'Right.' I didn't feel much wiser.

'Why?' Jenny was painfully curious. 'What did you see?'

'The...' I paused. I didn't know. 'The dream. It was Billy. Sasha was... hurting him.'

Jenny shrugged. 'Sasha does that. She is not kind to her child.'

'What?' I cried, horrified. 'Was that really happening?'

Jenny nodded. 'She is cruel. He has to be repaired heaps.'

'Repaired? But she was scalding her son!' I cried.

Jenny sighed. 'We do not interfere.' Her eyes were so sad.

'I bloody will interfere,' I snapped. 'We have to help him! I am fed up of this bloody place. Come on Rhys. We're going over there. Now.'

'But I've only just...' he started. Then he saw the look in my eyes. Red Alert. 'Fine.'

'It is OK. I will look after the baby,' offered Jenny.

I smiled at her, gratefully. If wishes were horses, I'd just got myself a stallion.

'Thanks.' I clasped her hands, briefly. 'Don't worry, you won't break her. There's a bag of nappies over there. Mind out for your clothes in case she goes all Banksy on them.' I threw Rhys's jacket at him. 'Come on.'

We were too late. Kind of.

Sasha's door was open, the lights were on. She was upstairs, curled up on the floor of the bathroom, sobbing. 'He wouldn't cry, he just wouldn't cry,' she whispered to herself.

Billy lay in the bath, lobster pink, like he had sunburn. His eyes were shut but he was still breathing.

I touched him, ever so gently. He shuddered, and let out a tiny moan. His skin... His skin felt wrong. Like it was lifting and melting under my touch. His eyes snapped open. 'It hurts,' he muttered. 'Is Mother still cross with me?'

Sasha roused herself from her corner. 'I am not your mother!' she spat.

We dragged Billy out, ever so gently, terrified that the skin would fall off him.

'I'm so sorry,' I cradled him carefully in my arms. I emptied the bath and stuck him under the shower, turning cool water on him gently. It was all I could think of. He shuddered, twitching terribly.

Rhys rang 999, called an ambulance and went hunting for bandages.

I stood in the shower with Billy, holding him like he was made of snow. Sasha stayed on the floor, ignoring us, whimpering to herself.

'Mother,' asked Billy, 'why do you not like me?'

'You are nothing to do with me!' she screamed, standing up and going downstairs. I found out later she'd poured herself a drink and microwaved a meal. I'd like to say she'd gone into shock... but I don't know. People are really, really odd. That's the only way to put it.

The ambulance never came. Instead there was a knock at the door. Sasha didn't bother opening it – she was watching television and turned the volume up. I could hear the strange applause and laughter of some stupid pointless show. Rhys went down and answered the door. People came upstairs. It was Tom and a woman.

'Bloody hell,' said Tom, staring in horror at Billy's blistering flesh.

The woman made a noise and started cursing.

'We're here to look after him,' she said, gently, professionally. 'We know what to do.' Her voice had a strong American twang. Funny how when Americans sound pissed off, they sound more pissed off than anyone else on the planet. She looked at me, and climbed under the shower with us, unfazed by the water on her clothes. Of all things, she smiled. 'Hi, you must be Gwen. It's nice to meet you. I'm Eloise.'

'You must be from the airbase,' was all I could think of saying. 'Tell me you've come to help him.'

She nodded. Then she dismissed me and gently, ever so gently, took Billy out of my arms. 'Come on you,' she said, her voice low and motherly. 'Come on baby, we're going to look after you.'

'Where are you taking him?' I demanded.

Tom shot me a look that said, 'Not Now,' but I stood my ground. Well, actually, I stood under a shower, fully clothed, holding a sodden towel.

'We're taking him home,' said Eloise, helping me onto the dripping floor.

'I'm coming with you,' I said very firmly.

Eloise paused, looking me up and down. 'You

want to see it, don't you?'

'Yes.'

We carried Billy into the back of the jeep. The garden path was a startling sight. It was lined with Scions. All stood at a distance. Mute. Sad. Watching us. They'd known.

Rhys followed me out. He'd brought out some blankets. He spread them out in the back of the jeep, and we lifted Billy in.

'Will he be OK?' Rhys asked me.

'I'm going to find out,' I told him.

He shook his head, but said, 'Fine.' It wasn't his most convincing. I knew what he was thinking. *It's starting all over again.*

'Please,' I said. 'I have to make sure he's all right.'

'Is that all?' Rhys asked. Eloise climbed into the front of the car, and Tom edged closer.

'Of course,' I said. 'I just want to make sure.'

Rhys shook his head again, sadly. 'Saving the world.'

'Make sure Anwen's OK,' I told him, and climbed into the back of the jeep with Billy. Because I was going to look after him.

The jeep started up, and I saw Rhys there, with the Scions standing behind him. All of them, blankly watching us go.

Eloise drove us over the bumpy roads like she was driving on cotton wool. Billy was shaking. Tom and I didn't speak.

We pulled up at the Weather Station, driving up to the gates. Standing there was a man. A really familiar man. He looked early twenties, but I'd seen him somewhere before. He was wearing a suit.

'Sebastian,' cried Eloise. 'Help me with him.'

The man called Sebastian stepped forward, picking Billy up and carrying him like he was made of tissue.

'Right then.' Eloise stuck her hands on her hips. 'We're going to find you some dry clothes, Gwen.'

'Where's Billy gone?' I asked a few minutes later. Inside the building looked like an office from an old film. Ancient computers spun reels of tape backwards and forwards while an old printer chugged out a long serpent of paper.

This was Eloise's kingdom. She smiled, like it was a brilliant and exciting thing.

'I'll show you around, Gwen. It's what you'd like, isn't it? Well, you're part of this now. Come on. Let's go and look at the hangar.'

I was being shown into a private world. The last time someone had said that to me, it was a tall, handsome man in a military greatcoat. I suddenly missed my old life.

Eloise swung open the door of the hangar.

Oh. Oh my god.

Rhys

I remember taking the baby to meet Gwen's folks.

We meet in a service station car park. That's how we roll these days. In the distance a motorway roars past. To the left are some truckers. To the right a load of shops that smell of farts.

In the middle, parked behind a camper van, Gwen introduces Anwen to her grandparents.

Gwen's mum Mary's dressed up for the occasion, even stuck on a new hat. She's crying a lot, and Gwen's dad is holding her shoulder, gripping it. He's wearing driving gloves (who wears driving gloves?) and we're not really saying that much. There is some talk about B-roads.

The traffic goes past, making that neow-neow-neow noise that traffic makes when you're playing at cars as a kid.

Mary's face has lit up, but she's crying so much as she holds that kid. Holds Anwen like she's something wonderful. Which she is. Gwen's leaning, just a little, back against the car. She's not quite steady on her feet, but she doesn't want to show it. She wants to seem so normal. She wants to say that everything is OK.

Which it is definitely not.

Geraint lets go of Mary. His hand eases off her shoulder gently. I imagine he changes gear like that. Ever so soft. He's a quiet man. I suspect the Cooper men all are. His glance is shifty, he wants to confide in me, and we step just slightly away from the three generations of Cooper Women.

We are standing next to someone else's mobile home.

'The mileage on these things always worried me,' he says.

I agree with him. There's little you can do other than agree with Geraint. He's never really held an awkward opinion in his life. He's never really disapproved of me, but then he's never really approved of me, either. He just gives me that little, nearly shy smile, like we're two people with the same problem, or the same brilliant secret. Gwen Cooper.

'How was it?' he asks. I'm guessing he means the birth.

'Bloody horrible,' I say. I don't go into detail.

'Right enough,' he grins.

We both pull a face. He sucks his teeth in. Like we're talking about a plumbing bill and not the miracle of childbirth.

'How is she?'

'Tired. Brilliant.'

'Good,' he says. He casts a drifting eye over at Anwen. 'Bit tiny, isn't she?'

'She'll grow up quick,' I say.

'Right,' Geraint nods. 'Gwen was a big baby.'

'Oh.'

'They do grow up. Takes you by surprise.'

We talk like that for a bit. Baby chit-chat. I'm standing there, trying not to cast an eye around too obviously, making sure the camper van shields us from any CCTV, watching out for any big black cars gliding silently along the slip road. Anything really.

At any minute, they're coming for us. I know this. But maybe not now. Not in a service station. Not behind a camper van with an amusing bumper sticker.

'Proud?' asks Geraint suddenly.

Startled, I say nothing, and he studies me closely. Guardedly. For an instant, I think he's going to say something wise. But he just nods.

'Don't worry,' I say to him. 'We're safe now. We've left it all behind.'

Geraint doesn't blink. 'Have you?'

'I hope so,' I say. 'I bloody hope so.'

'For her sake?' he asks. Looking towards Gwen. Or Anwen. I'm not sure who.

But I know that we're starting a new life. I'm so bloody relieved about that. Sure, we'll be hiding in the shadows, but we'll be safe. Anwen will be safe.

Gwen

The hangar was full of a vast and growing plant, spilling from a bed of mulch into the furthest corners of the room. It twisted and stretched like something impossibly wonderful in Kew Gardens. Yet it was here, in a dark and draughty hangar in North Wales.

'We call it the Juniper Tree,' said Eloise. 'You know, after those fairy tales where babies are found lying under Juniper Bushes.'

'Yes... but what is it?'

Eloise smiled. 'Would you believe me if I told you it was alien?'

I nodded.

'Very good. That saves us some time. Well, it's more than alien. It's an alien spaceship. Of sorts. Or the remains of one. We don't quite know. I think...' Eloise had warmed to her subject, and was leaning back against a bench. 'Many years ago we sent the *Voyager* probes out into space – complete with a little primer about the human race. Some drawings, a bit of art, maths and a few seeds. So that maybe, just maybe, if another alien species encountered us... they would know us. I think this is like that. Another species' version of a probe. Or what they'd send back. This –' she gestured at the vast plant – 'is their way of saying hello.'

I stared at the plant. 'Hello,' I said.

'Yeah,' drawled Eloise, nodding. 'But what a greeting! It's a viable, intelligent organism. When it landed... well, it was tiny. But from an acorn grew all this... And it became, well, an institution acquired it, and gave it to your government. They discovered what it could do. It makes the Scions, Gwen. The good Lord above knows how or why, but it does. What are little girls made of? Sugar spice and all things nice.'

'Slugs and snails and puppy dog's tails,' I finished.

We smiled at each other.

'My life is a bit odd,' laughed Eloise. 'But it's kinda beautiful.'

We stood in that room, looking up at the plant. I'm not sure for how long. It invited you to just stare at it, like the first snowdrops in spring, or a budding rose about to push out its first flower. You could almost see it growing. Eloise walked around it, telling me how she could even use it to talk to the Tree's home species. 'But what would we say to them?' she laughed.

'Is it anything to do with the stink thistles?' I asked.

Eloise nodded, approvingly. 'No one quite knows what they are. When they first started showing up, we were quite worried that they'd grow into more Juniper Trees. But they don't. They never do much – don't even flower. We tried getting rid of them and they just grew back.'

'How did it all start?' I asked. My voice was quiet, almost a whisper, like I didn't want to disturb the plant.

She shrugged. 'I think, like all government

projects, the origins are lost in a muddle of paperwork and balls-up. All I know is that someone, somewhere, got me in a few years ago to take charge.'

'What had gone wrong?'

'Oh, nothing really.' Bullshit. Eloise was a bad liar. She was evasive, her gaze sliding off anything rather than look you in the eye. 'Just... well, it was quite an undertaking.'

'But why does the plant make the children?'

Eloise clapped her hands together. 'Oh there's the question. Maybe just because it wants to.'

'Yeah, but... but why are you letting it do it?'

Eloise's smile faded a bit. 'This is a village without children. We are giving them—'

Yeah, yeah, yeah. 'The next best thing. But why are you doing it?'

Eloise looked away.

'Come on, let's see how poor Billy is doing.'

He was lying on a cold slab, wrapped in leaves. Leaves from the plant. His skin was no longer horrifically blistered, but instead a ghostly pale.

The calm and collected Sebastian was walking around the body, painting a thick green paste on the kid's flesh.

'What's that?' I asked.

'Pulp from the stink thistle plant,' he answered. 'It is stimulating the healing process and should stave off any long-term damage to the tissue.'

I stared at him. Handsome. Neat. Professional. Utterly artificial.

'You're a Scion!' I realised.

'Yes.' He didn't look up from brushing the paste on like it was gold leaf.

'But you're not a child.'

'No. I am older.'
'But how much older? The kids don't grow up…'
'Not at the normal rate. I am 30 years old.'
'So what's your story?'

Sebastian

I woke up on 3 March 1981. I could see the *date* on a *calendar* on the *wall*. The *room* was *white* and *smelt* of *disinfectant*. It was *bright, lit* by *electricity*. I was lying on a *metal table*. Standing over me was a *woman*. She was *smiling*.

'Well, that went rather well,' she said.

'Good morning,' I said to her, pleased with how my voice sounded.

She shook her head. Wrong. 'It is afternoon.'

'I see,' I said. I did not yet understand. 'Why am I here?' I asked her.

'That's what we're both going to find out.'

Her name was Elena Hilda Al-Qatari, although she never used her middle name. She was 36 years of age and from a place called Iran. She had studied at the University of Cambridge before coming here. 'Here' was, she admitted, 'going to take some explaining'.

'Can I get off this table?' I asked her.

'Are you going to kill me?' she replied.

I considered. 'No. Why would I want to do that?'

'Oh, you might,' she said. 'We just don't know.'

'What do you mean?' I asked her.

'We're different from you. So very different.'

Again, I paused.

'Why? Is it because we have differently coloured skin? Is that it? Does your darker skin mean that you are superior to me, or that I am superior to you?'

She laughed. She had a rich, deep laugh. 'No, no, it's not that.'

'Is it that we are different genders, then? Which is superior?'

Again, she laughed. 'Oh I like you,' she said. 'Don't change.'

'But Elena, I am already changing. I am constantly changing. In the last 173 seconds I have learned 84, 85, 86 new concepts. Some of these concepts are beginning to interconnect, creating further new concepts. Is there a finite number of concepts for me to know? Tell me… How far apart are the places Cambridge and Iran?'

'Several thousand miles and about a hundred years,' she sighed, then frowned. 'No, ignore that. I was being frivolous.' She saw my face. 'Wait. Frivolous… It means that some of the information I told you then was not accurate but was intended humorously.'

'Why would you convey inaccuracy?'

'Because… because sometimes that is what we do as a species. Sometimes it is for humour, or for self-protection, or to manipulate or to deceive. To cover up our own ignorance.'

'I see. So many ideas. Then what piece of your statement was correct?'

'I'm not going to tell you,' she grinned. 'You're going to have to work that out for yourself.'

'That is harder.' I frowned.

'People are hard. You're going to have to learn that if you're going to become one.'

'I see. So I am not a person?'

'I don't know. You're… you're very new.'

'I am 205 seconds old. You are 36 years old. That means that you must know so much more than me.'

She stuck her hands in her pockets. 'Come on, you,' she said. 'Get down off that table. Let's see if you can walk.'

I spent the next 413 seconds learning how to walk. She said that I was a fast learner. I told her that she was a good teacher. She told me that I had learned one of the basic arts of polite conversation: the exchange of mutual compliments.

'So what am I?'

'You are an artificial construct. We found an elaborate extraterrestrial organism that was capable of creating a synthetic life form. We learned how to programme it with datasets. We were able to give it all the information necessary in order to create a synthetic humanoid. You are our first attempt.'

'I see,' I said. 'Someone was able to give it all that information? Whoever could do that would have to be very intelligent indeed.'

She smiled. 'Thank you, you're very kind.'

'Yes.' I smiled back. 'Now it is your turn to say something nice about me.'

A few days later, I had a visitor. Elena had taught me to say 'a few' instead of the exact time. She said that imprecision was *a good thing in conversation*.

The visitor was a man in a long coat. He was very handsome in that his features were very symmetrically arranged and in a pleasing proportion to each other, making him physically attractive. I could tell that Elena thought this as well, as I could now read her body language and some of her thoughts. I wondered what this man's thoughts were.

'Cheeky,' said the man, wagging a finger at me.

'What?' I was innocent.

He shot a glance at Elena. 'You know he's telepathic, right?'

Her eyes widened with surprise. 'Why didn't you tell me...?' Her tone was accusing.

'Can't you read my thoughts?' I asked her. In truth, I had suspected that she could not. But I had known that this was a secret. I liked having a secret.

The man sat down. He had very neat hair and clear blue eyes. 'Hello,' he said. 'My name is Jack.'

'Hello,' I replied. 'I have no name.'

'Really?' He turned to Elena. 'We should do something about that, shouldn't we?'

She pulled a face at him. She was annoyed, I could tell. 'Sebastian,' she said after some thought.

'Really?' said Jack.

'Sebastian,' she repeated. 'Unless, that is...'

'No,' I said. 'I very much like the name. I am Sebastian.'

'Lovely,' said the man called Jack. 'So, Sebastian, why are you here?'

'I am afraid I do not know. No one has told me,' I said. And I was telling him the truth this time.

'Ah, well.' He looked cross. 'Do you... do you know where you come from?'

'I've asked him all this!' protested Elena.

'Yeah,' Jack puckered his lips. 'But I'm charming. He may have been keeping something back.'

'I am not keeping anything back.'

'Right.' Jack looked at Elena and me. 'Right then.' He stood up. 'It's been very nice meeting you, Sebastian.' He nodded to Elena.

*

He came back a few months later.

'Hello Sebastian, it's your Uncle Jack. How are you?'

'I have learned to read and write in both English and Arabic,' I said proudly. 'I have also a basic understanding of geometry, algebra, geography and contemporary history.'

'Right.' Uncle Jack pulled a face. 'Have you, by any chance, learned to fire a gun yet?'

'No,' I said. 'What is a gun?'

'I see.' Uncle Jack looked cross. 'Let me just have a word with Elena.'

He left. I could hear them shouting.

Later, Elena came into the room. She was carrying a strange object. 'Sebastian,' she said, haltingly. 'This is a gun.'

I picked it up. It was quite heavy and made of metal. 'What is it for?'

She hesitated. 'It is for proving that you can point at a target from a distance. If you can mark that target then you are very clever. That is what the gun is for.'

She pinned up a set of circles on the far wall and handed me the gun. She showed me how to point it. She explained that it would be very loud. I told her I understood. Then I pointed the gun and pulled back on the trigger. It stung my hands and made a very loud noise.

I had marked the very smallest circle right in the centre.

'Did I do it right?' I asked.

Elena looked unhappy. But she said, 'Yes, Sebastian, you did very well.'

'I see,' I said. 'I would like to do it again. Please

can I?'

The next time I saw Uncle Jack, he was very pleased with how I used the gun.

'It is odd,' I said to him. 'The force used by the bullet is much stronger than that required to penetrate paper. It is quite wasteful. I have some theories as to how the bullet could be replaced with wet paper soaked in ink, or even a small ball of paint. It would be much better, I think.'

'Very good,' said Uncle Jack. Now it was his turn to look unhappy.

This time, when he shouted at Elena, I could see what they were talking about through the glass door. Although I could not hear their words, I had learned to lip read. I was also able to work out some of what Elena was thinking.

'That is just a child, Jack!' she was screaming.

'All the same...' Jack was trying to be reasonable. He laid a hand on her shoulder, and she angrily shrugged it off.

'A child! You want me to make that child into a killer!'

'No, no,' said Uncle Jack. 'I don't want this. I'm just the messenger.'

'You're just obeying orders?' Elena's tone was quite strange.

'Don't be like that. You were put in charge of the Juniper Project to see what it could produce. It's been more successful than we could possibly have hoped. But obviously, there are people who are seeking a practical application. A return on their investment. That beautiful creature in there... it's not exactly a whole person is it? If we could take him, train him up... don't you see the possibilities?'

'I can see,' said Elena, slowly and sadly, 'that you like killing.'

'Not at all.' Uncle Jack was still using his 'being reasonable tone'.

'But… we still don't know what kind of creature… what Sebastian really is. Whether he's just a… pupal stage.'

'What do you mean?' Jack was curious.

'He might just look like a human. He may be about to revert to his parents' true form. Or transcend it.'

'What?'

'Oh come on. The Juniper Tree… it grows a version of the life form perfectly adapted to this planet. Maybe as an intermediary stage. Then perhaps it evolves, becoming something a bit more… like its real parents.'

'Oh.'

'Yes. And maybe its parents aren't as benevolent or as sweet as Sebastian. Maybe training him up to be a soldier and giving him weapons will one day seem like a very, very stupid idea.'

There was a long silence from Uncle Jack. I wondered how much of this Elena considered to be the truth.

'Well, Jack?'

'It wasn't my idea.' Uncle Jack's voice had a hurt tone. 'I suspect they try and turn everything we give them into weapons.'

'Including a child?'

'OK. OK. Well… listen. Maybe… maybe I'll come back when he's grown up a bit. Then we'll see.'

After he'd gone, Elena taught me about fairy stories. She told me one she called 'Jack and the Beanstalk'. It was about how you should never make promises to wicked uncles. And how you should be careful about magic seeds.

When I next saw Jack it was several birthdays later: I was almost 10. Elena and I had been working together for all that time.

Elena looked older. Jack and I looked just the same.

She was cross and worried, I could tell. She had started biting her fingernails. She left the room as soon as he arrived.

'Nice suit,' he said as I greeted him. I handed him a cup of coffee. He smiled. 'I get handed a cup of coffee by a handsome young man in a nice suit. I could get used to that.'

We smiled at each other. Warmly. I made sure of it.

Uncle Jack sat down in a chair, stretching out, his arms behind his head. He was pretending to be relaxed, I could tell. All the time he was watching me. Elena had shown me pictures of animals. I liked lions and tigers the most.

When Uncle Jack spoke it was with the same predatory casualness. 'OK then, my little man,' he said. 'Would you like some friends?'

'Not particularly.'

'Well, ah, you're going to get some.'

'I see.'

'You will like them. They're going to work with Elena. To watch over you. To give you tests and exams. To train you. You'll like that, won't you?'

'I like sums and geography and the poetry of Philip Larkin.'

Jack snorted with laughter. 'Read the one about

parents?'

'Yes,' I said.

'It's true, you know.' Jack stood, going to the door. 'Anyway. Your new friends will be here soon. Thanks for the coffee.'

I did not like the soldiers.

'Who did that to you?' asked Uncle Jack the next time I saw him.

I shrugged. 'It was an accident.'

'You've learnt to lie?' Uncle Jack growled. He reached out to touch the bruise on my face, but I stayed his hand. I did not flinch. I had learned not to flinch.

'Why, Elena, why?' shouted Uncle Jack.

Elena was standing in the corner, gnawing at her thumb. Her hair was untidy. She had not washed it for several days and I could smell it. She did not say anything. She had become very quiet since the soldiers came.

'The soldiers say they are teaching me to be a man, sir. They say I need to learn to fight back. They say this is fun. I do not think it is.'

'No.' Uncle Jack's voice was low. Angry. He turned back to Elena. 'How could you let this happen?'

Elena spoke. 'You're blaming me? How can you blame me? This was your bloody idea.'

'No.' Jack shook his head. 'I'm just the middle man. I'm just—'

'Obeying orders.' Elena kicked a chair.

Jack turned back to me. 'Sebastian, how often does this happen?'

I shrugged. 'A few times.'

'Don't give me that.'

'I try and stop it,' shouted Elena. 'I try. When I'm around. I come in early and stay late. But they won't let me stay overnight. It's a security risk, apparently. And when I'm not around… they… they do what they like to him.'

'You should have told me,' snapped Jack.

'How? I don't have your phone number.'

'Good point.' Uncle Jack groaned. He pressed his hands to his face. 'Sometimes… sometimes I get it very badly wrong.' He spread his fingers, peeping out at me. 'Sebastian. I would like you to believe me when I say that I am very sorry for what has happened to you.'

'I am sorry, too. I have made Elena sad, I have let you down, and I have made the soldiers angry.'

Uncle Jack patted me on the shoulder and stood up. 'Shaddup,' he said. He turned around. 'I'm off to do a bit of shouting.'

Uncle Jack came back in the night. I woke up to find him standing over my bed.

'Now then,' he said. 'I've just had a crazy idea. We can't keep the two of you here.'

'What do you mean?' I asked. 'Where is Here? No one has ever explained that to me. Is it near Cambridge?'

'No time for new concepts,' he said. 'You and Elena are going on a holiday.'

'What's a holiday?'

Uncle Jack shook his head. 'It's fun. You get to do it by following me very quietly down the corridor. If you do it right, you never get to see the soldiers again.'

'I would like to go on holiday, please.'

'OK then,' said Uncle Jack.

We walked down the corridor, further than I had ever been. Along it were some of the soldiers. They were lying down and having a sleep in uncomfortable positions. Behind a door was the sound of banging and shouting.

'What is that? That sounds like Sergeant Evans. He does not sound happy that we are going on holiday.'

'No.' Uncle Jack smiled.

I could hear gunshots behind the door. The door jumped.

'They're shooting at the lock,' said Jack.

'Is it a hard target to hit?' I asked.

'No,' said Uncle Jack, grabbing my shoulder. 'I think we should run.'

We stood outside. I had been outside before, occasionally, but never at night. I could see stars and I began to count them, but Uncle Jack said that was the wrong thing to do at this time. But the 137 that I was able to count were very beautiful. He pulled out a gun and continued to drag me along, towards what I knew was a jeep. Inside it sat Elena. She ran out to hug me.

Behind us, there was noise and shouting and gunfire.

'Target practice?' I asked. Elena held me close.

'That's right,' said Uncle Jack. 'But they're rubbish. I'm better.' He fired his own gun. I was interested to see that a couple of soldiers fell to the ground, crying out, clearly pleased that Jack had hit them.

'You are very good,' I said.

'Yes, I am,' said Uncle Jack. 'But I'm a very bad driver.'

We were still climbing into the jeep when Uncle Jack began to drive off. Bullets flew around us, but Elena held me down on the floor of the jeep, against a black rubber mat and a blanket that smelt of damp and wool.

We drove on into the night.

It was a while before anyone spoke.

'About this holiday,' began Uncle Jack. 'I was just wondering if you'd like some brothers and sisters.'

'No!' shouted Elena.

'Oh come on,' sighed Uncle Jack. 'He's reached his tenth birthday without growing a single tentacle or slaughtering anyone. Do you know how much it was costing us in guards?'

'I am very sorry,' I said, 'Have I wasted your money? Elena gives me pocket money. I can lend you that.'

Jack smiled. 'No, no. Please don't. I was just thinking... freedom. The chance to do something really wonderful.'

Elena and Jack and I went to our new home. It was called Rawbone. We travelled in the jeep. I was very excited by the jeep. I was very excited by the open air. I was very excited by spending my money on chocolate and sweets in a shop on the way. ('Don't eat them all at once,' said Jack, 'or you'll be sick.') I bought 500 Milk Bottles, as they are my favourite sweet.

'Can I have 300 Yellow ones and 100 White and 100 Pink?' I asked the lady. She said no. But I still got 500 Milk Bottles.

I ate 83 of the milk bottles on the journey and was not sick.

We drove into Rawbone. It was a small village.

Almost certainly the smallest village we had driven through. It welcomed careful drivers. Jack was not a very careful driver. Elena did not travel well.

We came to our home.

Jack said it would be a safe place to have a holiday. No one would come looking for us here and we could do valuable work and the Juniper Tree would arrive soon.

The safe place to have a holiday had a sign outside saying 'Weather Monitoring Station'. Inside it was big, and very cold.

'No central heating, yet,' said Jack. 'I'm hoping to get that fixed.'

'You'd better,' warned Elena. 'Before the Juniper Tree arrives. If it dies of cold, I won't be responsible.'

'Don't worry. Now then...' Jack sank down slightly, as he did when he talked to me, bending his knees just a bit to look me in the eye. 'Would you like to see the sea, Sebastian? I bet you've never seen anything like it before.'

Uncle Jack and I stood on a cliff, looking down at the sea and out at the sunset, which was taking place apparently twenty-one miles away. I figured this was almost correct, but I rather suspected the mathematical principles used to calculate this.

'It is very nice,' I said.

'Come on!' said Uncle Jack. 'This is your first sunset, your first glimpse of the sea. Not a new tea towel. It is not nice. It is beautiful, it is amazing. It is not *nice*. Nice is for small things.'

'Like tea towels.' I did not know what a tea towel was.

'Yes.' Uncle Jack smiled. 'Now then. Why are you here, Sebastian?'

'I do not know.'

'Then let me give you a purpose. These people. The people of the village we drove through... they are very sad because they cannot have children. Do you understand that?'

'Yes,' I said. 'Yes I think I do.'

'Well, would you like to do something to help them?'

'Yes,' I said. 'But I do not know if I can.'

'Oh I think you can.' Uncle Jack rubbed my shoulder. 'I think you can help give them the children they want. You'd be doing a good thing.'

'And if I didn't? Would I have to go back to the soldiers?'

Uncle Jack shook his head. 'I don't think so.' He shrugged evasively. 'I'll sort something out.'

We stood there, watching the sun set.

I wondered if it would rise again. Jack said that it did this every day, but it seemed impossible.

Elena and I liked our new home very much. So did the Juniper Tree, which I tended and fed and watched grow. Every day it had new leaves and shoots. Eventually it budded.

In case the people of Rawbone became curious, Elena suggested that I start calling her Mother. So I did. I liked that.

Mother and I took delivery of some computers. They were wonderful but slow. I learned how to programme them, and they watched the Juniper Tree when we were sleeping. Mother started to sleep more and more.

We worked to give children to the people of Rawbone. Children modelled initially on me. We were making people happy. It was a good holiday. It lasted many years. I felt pleased with our work.

One day, Mother came to see me. She was tired, even though she had slept a lot the night before. 'Sebastian,' she said. 'I'm going away for a while.'

'Oh,' I said. 'Are you having a holiday from our holiday?'

She paused for a second. 'Yes.' She spoke as though she had something in her throat. 'I am.'

'Will you come back?'

Again she paused. But she told me that she would come back. If she could. She explained that she had had to make a lot of arrangements, but that she hoped that it would all be all right. She hoped I would not be lonely.

'I will miss you,' I said. 'I love you.'

'Do you?' she asked, peering at me intensely. 'Do you love me?' She made the same odd sound in her throat and brushed something from her eyes.

I nodded. I loved her. I think I did. Or at least I knew that telling her this made her happy.

'You are beautiful and amazing,' I told her.

She smiled, and rubbed my hair. 'Oh, Sebastian,' she sighed, 'I love you very much.'

She hugged me and I noticed that she had lost weight.

I got a new mother. Her name was Eloise.

Eloise was nice. But Eloise was not very happy. She received a lot of emails that made her cross and angry.

'Is there anything I can do?' I asked her.

She looked at me. Hard.

'No,' she said. 'I don't think there is. Sorry, Sebastian. But thanks for trying.'

Rhys

Oh god.

I got back to the caravan and it was empty. No Jenny. No Anwen.

I spent a couple of seconds thinking nice normal don't-panic thoughts. Like the two of them were down the toilet block, maybe. Well, actually I ran there. No sign of them.

I looked around at the desolate caravan park. No pram. The pram had gone. No bloody pram marks. Maybe she was just taking the baby for a walk. At night. In the rain.

I pulled my mobile out. Force of habit. There was hardly ever a signal here. Occasionally you'd get the ghost of a single bar. Not this time – it was useless.

I needed Gwen. I needed to find our baby. I felt sick. I stood around the caravan, trying not to panic. But I *was* panicking. I decided that there are a couple of things in this world that you are allowed to panic about. One of them is when your baby goes missing.

When I was young, my mum was always losing me in shopping centres. No matter how many times she'd say 'stay there, by the stairs,' I'd always wander off. This was because shopping was dull, even then, and it was always much more fun to hide in the racks of clothes pretending they were a tepee. You're a selfish bugger when you're young, and if you're stood around in the Ladies section of M&S there's nothing to do. So of course you wander a bit. You'll get back there in the end.

The trouble I got in. The fury from my mother. Oh, she'd shout at me, clap me round the back of the neck, and order me never to do it again. But I would. Because shopping was boring. I once got so lost I got tannoyed. I was dead proud of that, but my mother was furious and ashamed. 'Never do that again,' she said, and burst into tears when we were back in the Chrysler.

I never really understood what the problem was. Until one day when I stood at home having lost my baby. Up until that moment I had known where my child was every second of every day. And now I didn't.

I ran up and down the lane. It wasn't exactly a coordinated search. It was more like panicky oh please god, oh please wandering. I wasn't coping well. I tried a few deep breaths, I tried taking stock, I tried making a bloody list, but none of it worked. My baby was missing and I felt too sick to think straight.

That's the odd thing about having a baby. Up until the birth, you know, I was... well, I was kind of mentally prepared and everything. I was pleased we were having a kid. I wanted to be a Good Dad. But that was it... you know, pleased as punch and dead proud... but no actual FEELINGS for it.

But as soon as the baby was born, as soon as I heard her crying and knew that Gwen was OK, as soon as I saw her... she upgraded my brain. Rhys 2.0. My mind was reprogrammed. Both Gwen and I were suddenly slaves to our dear little parasite. We were putty in her tiny hands. We put up with

the sleep deprivation, the
reams of grubby demands. b
And we would do anything for
the most important thing in th
dictator. Our world.

But then, just for a moment, we
off her. It would, of course, have to be
that bloody alien stuff. The life we though
behind. Gwen's life.

Just for an instant, I flared up with rage. Somehow
this was Gwen's fault.

But it wasn't.

With the loss of Anwen, everything about me
crumbled. I went from being Rhys Williams, proud
dad and loving husband, to just a very scared,
pathetic man sobbing in an empty country lane in
the rain. When you are an adult, you spend a lot of
time pretending to be a grown up. You're not really.
Everyone is still about 14. You just pretend you're
not. You drink beer, you talk about sex, you swear,
you buy a house, you have kids, you get a job... you do
everything you can to prove how grown up and adult
and important you are. But really, really, you're not.
You've no bloody idea how to live your life. You're
just doing what everyone else does in the hopes that
you're somehow doing it right. Shoring yourself up
against the real world. The world that was cruel and
terrible and took everything away.

But here I was and I knew I was doing it all
wrong.

Eloise

Things got interesting at that point.

Gwen Williams... Oh, she was tired, almost exhausted. If I'd been her doctor, I'd have sent her straight home to bed. But she was still pressing on. Yet underneath all of the bags and the puffy cheeks, her eyes were wide alert and intelligent.

You know something about stuff like this, I thought. You do. You're quite alert, lady.

She seemed unfazed about Sebastian's true nature. Intrigued. Not in an 'oooh blimey' way, more as though she'd put together a mental list of quite tough questions.

'So, how long have you two been in the village?' she asked. Question Number One. She'll know that we'll both give different answers. She listens as Sebastian says that he arrived in 1991. Quite innocent. Quite candid.

'After the children stopped being born?'

'Oh yes.'

'Right.' Question Number Two was brewing, somewhere. You could tell it was ticking away. Gently. Gently.

'Would you like a cup of tea?' asked Sebastian. 'Or coffee?' His unconcern about Billy lying in front of him... even I found it a bit chilling.

'What's going to happen to Sasha?' asked Gwen.

Ah, there it was.

Sebastian responded to this blankly, confused.

'Well, I would hope that... the authorities would want to...'

Gwen snorted. 'PC Wandering Hands? No chance. Poor cow. That woman is messed up. She needs proper help.'

'No, I quite agree, Mrs Williams,' I covered quickly. 'Sasha could have harmed her child very badly.'

Wrong thing to say. 'And her not being able to have her own child... might not have had something to do with it?' She looked at me. Full beam.

I rose up, aggressively firm. I was angry, angry with myself because I suspected that somehow... somehow we *were* to blame. 'No, no, no. It's a separate issue. And a lot of the parents have taken to their children very well. Overall the project is a success.'

'But why?' demanded Gwen. 'Why do it at all?' She glanced at Sebastian. 'I mean, no offence, but there's no need to have done this... unless... I mean, what's the real reason?'

'I don't know what you mean,' I said.

'Yeah,' snorted Gwen. 'But what about you, Sebastian? Why were you born? The children themselves don't know. What about you?'

'I don't know. But initially... I think the people who created me wanted me to be a soldier.'

Cat. Out. Of. The. Bag. Jeez.

Gwen boggled. Worried. 'What? I'm sorry, what?'

'Oh, that was the original nature of the experiment.' I tried to flap this away, but I felt a worried sense in my guts. Real worry.

There was no stopping Sebastian now, though. 'Oh yes. They discovered the tree, and saw in it a seed bank. It is how my race visits other planets –

a seed bank lands and learns all it can about the environment before germinating a seed, growing a creature that can survive on the planet that it has landed on.'

'So you don't really look like this?'

Sebastian looked puzzled. 'I... I do. But my own species has no form of its own. We spread through the universe like... dandelions on the breeze.'

'Yeah.' Gwen looked sceptical. 'Dandelion soldiers?'

'No,' said Sebastian. 'That was the idea of man. They worked out how to manipulate the coding of the gene bank before they activated it. I was the prototype.' Suddenly he seemed sad. 'I am a disappointment. I am no good at killing.'

I walked Gwen back to her car. I could see her anger, but I headed it off. I didn't really feel like any confrontation. None at all. I was dog tired. We both were. She looked so exhausted she might cry.

'You're growing soldiers.' Her alarm was clear. Put like that, it sounded really bad. But then again, she didn't know the full story.

'Yeah.' I took time over my breath. Keep casual. 'Some cockamamie idea. Some bright spark realised the Scions were a synthetic life form. They could be easily controlled. Made subservient. Perfect little disposable soldiers.'

Gwen stared at me.

'But don't worry – they got the mix wrong with Sebastian, bless him. He's as docile as a kitten. Of course, nowadays we understand so much more about the DNA helix, but back then it was like sewing with a chisel.'

Lights came on the road up ahead of us. A car engine driven badly to the gates. For an instant I flinched – what if this was an attack? What would we do?

Instead the car stopped at the fence. One of the Scions, Peter, was driving. His mother, Mrs Harries, got out and started waving at us frantically. Calling out Gwen's name. Over and over.

Gwen started running towards her. On impulse.

How did she know? They say animals know when it's time for them to die. They say twins know what each other are thinking. But what genetic fluke was it that told Gwen that someone had stolen her baby?

Gwen

They took me to Rhys.

I was fairly sure I'd stopped screaming by that point, but the wrinkles in his face told me that just maybe I hadn't. I didn't know whether to hit him or hug him, but he risked a hug anyway, grabbing me and holding me while I shouted at him.

It felt almost all right. Being with him. But still I felt alone. Like I wasn't complete. A bit of me wasn't just missing, it had been ripped out like a handful of hair.

'Jenny,' said Rhys.

He had to say it a couple of times. I just wasn't taking anything in. I was just shouting at him, demanding my baby back.

Eventually something made me stop and take it all in. Jenny. My head replayed all those moments. Her fascination with Anwen. Her desire to befriend us. Her eagerness to please. To hold her. She was a girl. She had been for a very long time.

I remembered what I was like at that age – if I wanted something, I went out and I got it. Didn't matter if it was a boy, a handful of stolen sweets, or some boots. Had to have 'em.

She had just wanted a bloody kid. So she stole one.

What a mess.

*

The village had gone into shock. Shock with pitchforks and torches. They looked like a Frankenstein mob, only they were scouring the countryside.

I was standing there, in the middle of the village green. Surrounded by men and women I'd never spoken to. They were squeezing my arm, saying stuff to me. Then going off, out into the night, to look for my baby. People are nice. But there was something more to it than that. The looks I'd seen before – the envy, the resentment, the jealous hatred – all replaced with something both noble and repellent – they saw me as more human now. Someone to be pitied and helped. Incomplete. Just like them.

Rhys came back. Which I guess meant he'd been away. Things were a bit jumpy.

'I'm cold,' I told him.

'Yeah, love,' he said, wrapping a blanket round me. 'You've been standing here for an hour.'

I balled a hand into my eyes. 'What time is it?'

'Doesn't matter,' he said. 'We're staying awake until she's found. We all are. The whole village.'

'I should never have left her with Jenny,' I said.

He looked away. 'It's OK.'

'No. No, it isn't.'

'We'll get her back.' Again he didn't look at me.

'We've got to find her.'

'Yes.' There was something in his voice. But I picked away at it. Provoking it. Until he finally snapped.

'This is your bloody fault!' He didn't raise his voice. It was worse. A quiet despair. 'Aliens. First you get dragged in, then you pull me in... but I never thought you'd include our daughter. You promised.'

'Yeah,' was all I could manage, and even that hurt.

He was so right, I was furious and wanted to punch him. But I couldn't scream or shout. 'I promised. But I lied. We're never going to escape this.'

'No,' Rhys growled like an angry dog. 'We're getting her back. Then we're leaving. No more of this. Torchwood is dead. Let someone else pick up the pieces. Look what it's cost us.'

'Everything,' I said without thinking.

Rhys didn't say anything more.

Mrs Harries came up to us, holding tumblers.

'Brandy,' she said. 'That's supposed to be good for shock. But I got this whisky from Mrs Meredith ages back. Hoped the kids would have a crack at it. But no. Bloody saints. Anyway, give it a go.' She pressed the glass into my hands and I swigged at it. I didn't even feel it burn.

'Where are the children?' I asked.

She looked away, reticent. Suddenly I was the one to tiptoe around. 'In the village hall. I got Peter and Paul to round them all up and take them there. I didn't want them left hanging around. Not after what happened earlier.'

I stood there. Trying to say something. Nope. I had nothing.

She tutted, and looked unguardedly annoyed with me. 'I know it's not your fault, love, but it's all falling apart. None of this would have happened... None of it...'

Not if I hadn't come to Rawbone. I knew what she meant. But I just couldn't agree.

'This was never going to work. Not in the end.'

'But we were trying so hard.' Her voice a frustrated whine, Mrs Harries turned away from me, walking off towards the village hall. 'You make me realise how much I've lost, Gwen,' she said. 'Drink your whisky and come with me. We'll get your baby back.'

The Scions were standing in a circle. They looked almost sullen and truculent. None of them met my eye. I guessed they were picking up on the mood of the village, soaking it in like a sponge.

I walked up to one of them. 'It's Peter, isn't it?'

'Good evening, Mrs Williams,' he said. His eyes were stuck to the floor, sullen. He was almost like a proper teenager now. 'I am sorry about your baby.'

'Yeah,' I said, gently. 'I was just wondering – what can you tell us about Jenny?'

Peter shrugged. A movement that was echoed around the Scions like a rippling Mexican wave of don't-know-don't-care.

'Peter.' Use their name, keep using their name. You'll get through to them eventually. You'll win them over. Just keep using their name. 'The thing is, Peter, I know you're not normal children. And that's OK. Believe me, it is.'

'Yes,' he said. If he could have said 'yeah', I really think he would have.

'Listen,' I urged, 'it's OK. I don't blame any of you for what happened.' That was a lie, but desperation pushed it out. 'I just need your help. You're… you're telepathic, aren't you?'

Peter looked up. The others looked up. 'Not exactly,' muttered another of the children.

'Well, then, look, I don't quite know the word. It's not important – but you're all linked aren't you? You knew when Billy was hurt.'

'Yes,' said another Scion.

'Did you feel it?' Mrs Harries was holding Paul

by the shoulder. She was concerned. What Billy had suffered – she was horrified at the idea that it had echoed out through all the children.

Paul nodded, looking down at the ground. 'But we know that he will be fine now. He is recovering.'

'Yes,' Mrs Harries's voice was firm. 'Thanks to Mrs Williams. She left her baby behind to help Billy. And now she's lost her little girl because of that. Will you help her find her daughter?'

Nothing from the circle.

Mrs Harries slid her hand off her son's shoulder like it was cold stone. She walked over and held me. Gently. 'I'm sorry, Gwen,' she murmured. 'I just thought… I just thought they'd learned to be better than this.' She kicked out at the spindly leg of a plastic chair. 'I'm so sorry, dear. I sound so stupid. I'm just a stupid old woman. Silly.' Her voice cracked. I wondered what she'd have been like. If she'd been allowed to have children, to grow up properly. Not this strange steel wool mixture of desperation and hope.

'Come on,' she said, steering me towards the door. 'Let's leave them to it.'

We headed to the exit.

'Wait.' Peter's voice called back to us. 'Mother, please.'

Mrs Harries looked at me. Triumph flashed in her eyes. 'Gotcha,' she whispered.

Rhys

Gwen and I didn't speak much. We just held each other really tightly as we walked through the fields. We started off running, but after a while... well, there's only so much of that you can do. And she was exhausted. I felt utterly shattered. Like I just wanted to lay my head down on the sofa and sleep for a week.

How long was it since I'd had eight hours of pure sleep?

You know how it is when someone says, 'Ooh, I feel literally gutted.' Well yeah, that was how I felt. Literally. Exhausted. Empty. But also sick, deep inside. I was beyond worried and into this whole weird place. Where I just wanted to sleep.

My little head was running the same programme over and over again. It'll be OK. It won't be OK. Anwen will be waiting at home. You will never see Anwen again. It's all your fault. It's all Gwen's fault. Oh, I'll do anything just to get her back. Maybe, just maybe, that baby was ruining our life and we'd be better off without... No, don't think that last one.

If it wasn't for the worry, I could have used the peace to get a really good night's sleep.

Gwen squeezed my hand. Not 'I love you'. Just 'you're still here, and so am I'. Truthfully, she looked shocking. It wasn't just worry, although god knows, she looked ten years older. It was pain.

'You've not fed her, have you?'

Gwen shook her head, grimacing. 'All this milk. I feel like I'm going to burst.'

'It's OK, love,' I said. 'We'll see her in a minute.'

Platitude. Mistake. They never worked on Gwen. She scowled at me. 'We are traipsing through a bloody field at midnight, Rhys. She could be anywhere.'

'We're not on our own,' I said. 'The whole village is walking behind us.'

A hand tapped me on the shoulder. It was Peter. The Scion looked alert, his eyes flashing. 'She is over there... I think.' He gestured. 'She is on the beach.' He wrinkled his nose. 'The sea. And something else. Yes.'

Gwen came back to life. 'Leave it to us,' she said. Making the decision. But I really wanted her to. Somehow the world felt better with Gwen in charge.

The beach wasn't much. A figure was sat there in silhouette, crouched on a rock. Our shoes slapped on the wet sand as we ran towards it, but it just didn't seem to get any closer, a mirage in the desert.

'Anwen!' screamed Gwen. She was shouting as she ran. The sand was so rigid and hard beneath our feet and the figure so far away. But Gwen sounded so desperate.

Jenny looked up. Not startled, not frightened, threatening or ashamed. Blank. Puzzled in the moonlight.

'Hello, Gwen,' she said simply. She held up a little bundle. My bundle. Making little still-alive murmuring and whimpering noises of complaint. That's my girl.

There was a moment. A nasty moment. Gwen's hands were all claws and nails, and she made a noise

– a screech of pure rage. Just for that moment, it looked like she was going to shred Jenny. But she didn't. Mind you, I felt like knocking her block off.

Still furious, Gwen snatched our baby out of Jenny's arms like she was a rugby ball. Jenny didn't even put up a fight. She just continued to sit there. She didn't react.

Gwen and I held Anwen. She looked so pretty and contented, like she knew the secrets of universal happiness and would gradually forget them as she grew older. We just gloried in the moment. Then Anwen sensed milk and started to cry loudly. Normal service was resumed.

Gwen fed her. You know when you come in from a night out on the lash and the last two hundred metres you've been hopping from side to side desperate to pee, dancing with your keys and finally bolting in through the door and into the bathroom? That was pretty much the sound Gwen made. Pure amazed relief. Anwen made echoing gurgles of delight.

Jenny sat there. If anything she looked mildly disappointed. 'She was hungry,' she sighed, wistfully. 'I tried to feed her. But I couldn't.'

I started to shout at her then. Loudly. I was so cross. The louder I shouted the blanker Jenny became. Just less and less of her. Genuinely like shouting at a wall, a concrete wall – blank and grey, cold and solid. Her face upturned, looking at me, calm and casual and empty. Like she was just waiting for me to run out of steam. I wasn't going to. For the first time, I noticed she was wearing a beautiful flower in her hair – one of the stink thistles had bloomed.

'Rhys.' Gwen pulled me up, firm but gentle. She sat down on the rock next to Jenny. The two of them looked out to the sea.

When Gwen spoke, her voice was soft and encouraging. 'Jenny, why did you do it?'

The reply, when it eventually came, was so sad. 'I just wanted to grow up,' she sighed. The sea washed in, the sea washed out. 'I have been like this for twenty years. Not grown up. Never growing up. Always like this. I can feel my body changing, but too slowly. I would like to be an adult. I would like a child of my own. I figured if I had one, then maybe it would finally happen. I saw you with your baby and I thought that if I took it then I would grow up. That I would change if I had a baby.' She sounded wistful. 'I just wanted to be real.'

None of us said anything for a bit. We were all waiting for Jenny to finish, the silence punctuated by Anwen's gentle snuffling. Then Jenny continued.

'So I took your baby. But nothing happened. Nothing changed. I didn't grow up.' She sighed, and it was longest, saddest sigh. 'I am not real. I did not even feel anything. She was not mine.' She laid a hand on Gwen's shoulder, and Gwen didn't flinch. 'I am sorry that I caused you pain. I figured it would be worth it. I just did not think it through.'

Gwen looked at her and there was a little kindness at the edges of her lips and eyes. 'You didn't think it through. You just did something selfish and stupid and cruel. Because you felt like it.'

'Yes,' Jenny nodded.

And then Gwen said something quite remarkable. 'You're more human than you think, Jenny.'

Eloise

Hey Eloise

Just catching up, really. Thanks so much for your last report. I couldn't quite get the PDF to print, but I'm sure it's quite detailed and very thorough and up to your usual standard. So, well done you!

Running through the summary in your last email, a few things jumped out at me. Nothing we haven't spoken of before. But it certainly looks like you've had a busy few days!

One big thing is that the latest round of Efficiency Savings are beginning to bite, and it's up to me to ask projects to step up to the plate and deliver. It's time to kick the Rawbone Project into the next stage so that we can see some solid ROI. Sorry, but it seems painfully clear to me that the environment for the experiment is no longer tenable. Assaults and kidnapping tell me the balance between the Scions and the humans is broken beyond restoration. I've spoken to the higher ups and they all agree it's the right time to make this exciting move. I know it's a risk, but I genuinely think it will be brilliant.

So... I think, mebbe stop playing around and really change the gear on this one, ok?

Obv, totally up to you, but I really do think that's best, yeah? Your call!

Over to you,
xJasx

I read the email a few more times. I don't know what I'd expected it to say. I don't know, maybe somehow in my head, I'd hoped that Jasmine would just once… ease back. No. Instead she had, in her own unique way, ordered me to commit murder.

I sat in my chair, feeling sick. Sebastian had brought me a cup of tea a few minutes earlier. I couldn't bear to drink it.

I wondered about asking Tom for help. Of making this somehow his problem too. But that wasn't fair. It wasn't kind. And I also didn't want him to know what I was about to do.

I toyed with sending Jasmine a threatening, abusive reply. But I didn't want to do that, either. I speculated briefly if she really had all that much support in the office. An office I'd never even seen. I ran through all sorts of helpless, half-formed ideas. Protest. Refuse. Go over her head. But… I had no idea who was above her head.

The one thing I did not think, not out loud, was the terrible truth of my situation – that I was a weak woman about to do a terrible thing because I had no other choice. I balled my fists and drummed and drummed them against my legs. There was nothing else I could do, really.

Finally, when everything else was exhausted, I went to find Sebastian.

I passed Tom, who was engrossed in his PC. 'Anything I can do, boss?' he said, as sincere as a kid offering to help with the washing-up.

'No, it's OK. Farmville needs you more than I do.' I heard the crack in my voice.

'Cheeky arse,' muttered Tom as I left.

I found Sebastian looking after the printouts.

'We're almost out of paper,' he said. 'I will go and get a fresh ream.'

'It's OK, Sebastian,' I said. 'There's something else I'd like you to do.'

'All right,' he said, patient. 'Would you like something to drink?'

'No thanks,' I said. 'Can you come with me?'

We went through to the hangar, and stood in there. Sebastian always loved that room. It was hard to describe the effect it had on him, as he was always kind and pleasant, but he was at his most kind, most pleasant in that room, as though absorbing the warmth of the heat lamps. Involuntarily, his deep blue eyes shifted from me to the giant plant, adoringly.

'She looks so beautiful,' he sighed.

'She?' I asked.

'I think of her as she. Mothers are she, are they not?'

He turned to me, and smiled a radiant smile.

I pulled out a wheeled chair that had seen better days. 'Sit down, please,' I said.

He sat down without question, and waited patiently, staring up at the Juniper Tree. I crossed to a cupboard and reached for the equipment.

'Could you roll up your sleeve?' I said to him, and he complied, all the time smiling placidly at the giant plant. 'Now then, you'll feel a slight scratch,' I said, hoping my hand wasn't trembling too much.

'OK,' he said, but didn't even react as the needle pricked into his flesh. Soon I had the IV hooked up. For a second his gaze shifted, squinting as though trying to watch the plant through the distortion of the plastic tube with its gently dripping liquid.

Sebastian didn't ask why, he didn't question me. He never did. He simply sat there, smiling calmly. Until he blinked.

'It feels odd, Mother.'

'Don't call me that,' I snapped.

'I am sorry. It feels odd, though, Eloise.'

'Yes, I know,' I said, reaching out to stroke him. Then I hugged him, briefly. Feeling then how beautiful, how warm he was. There was a smell around him, like a freshly mown meadow. 'You're so wonderful,' I said to him. 'How do you feel?'

Sebastian reached out an arm, staring at his hand, first the back, then the palm, then the back again. 'My vision is remarkably clear,' he said.

I just stood there, gripping an empty plastic water cup, feeling how solid it was, but how fragile it was – if I gripped too tightly, it would break.

Sebastian continued sitting in the chair, examining his hand. 'Can I get you a cup of tea?' he asked, absently. His voice was thick and slurring. Suddenly the hand, the whole arm jerked up and spasmed. Then he fell silent.

When the end came it was very quick.

Sebastian gasped, his whole body sagging. His head fell back and his whole body slipped out of the chair, falling against the plant. I ran to his side, holding him.

'I am not well,' he whispered.

'It's OK, it's OK,' I told him. 'Oh baby, I love you, I love you.'

'I am so tired,' he said.

'Just rest. You've worked so hard. It's time for a break.'

'OK,' he said.

There was a noise. A whispering. I realised what it was. The leaves of the Juniper Tree were stirring and rustling. The branches were twisting.

Sebastian's eyelids fluttered. 'The plant... the plant is ill.'

'It will pass,' I assured him.

He struggled to sit up, but couldn't.

'Make sure the plant... the plant...' He stopped speaking, his lips formed into a little 'oh'.

Then his eyes closed and he sank back.

The rustling of the leaves stopped.

I crouched there for a while, holding him. Until I felt a cramp in my leg. So I stood up gently and walked away, wiping the tears from my eyes.

I left the hangar and walked across the wet tarmac, over to a small shed. The padlock was rusted and ice cold to the touch, sucking the feeling from my hand and I wrestled to get it open. For a moment I thought it wouldn't open, and I felt the rich irony – that I had taken a life, the life of someone I really cared for, and it had all been for nothing – that all Jasmine's plans would be frustrated because of a cheap old padlock. Suddenly the day seemed somehow better and easier. I'd just go back and email her. Tell her I'd tried. And that only Sebastian had known where the bolt cutters were. Sebastian...

The padlock opened at last, the hasp catching my knuckle. It stung, but I deserved it. I sucked it, opening the shed door. Inside it glowed the same greeny-blue as the Juniper Tree. But all that was in the shed was a single pod, sealed in bubble wrap and kept warm under a gently glowing sun lamp. There was a bench with a pair of scissors on it. Odd that. I was always running short of scissors, always losing them, always getting Sebastian to go and find me some. But I never came here.

I turned the sunlamp up to full heat. And waited.

Rhys

It was nearly dawn.

Josh and I sat outside the pub on a little wet bench. He sipped at a can of coke, and wearily checked his watch.

'Great. In three hours' time I have to go and cut the hair of some mildly racist old ladies. Hardly seems worth going to sleep.'

'No,' I said. 'Thanks for staying up. For helping.'

'Yeah,' Josh sighed. 'Bit of drama. Wouldn't have missed it for anything. Glad it worked out OK.'

'Me too,' I admitted. 'Just when I was starting to think I knew all the surprises a baby could offer.'

'Yeah.' Josh tipped the coke back. 'You must be shattered.'

'Beyond tired, mate,' I admitted.

I just wanted Gwen to get back from chatting to Mrs Harries. I didn't want to let Anwen out of my sight, but Gwen had said it was important. She wanted to thank the children. Well, wanted is the wrong word – she felt it was the right thing to do.

'Never fancied kids of your own?' I asked Josh.

He shook his head. 'Tom is more than enough child for me.'

'Where is he?' I asked.

'Working,' he murmured. 'They work odd hours... You know what the Weather is like.'

'I see,' I said.

'Funny really. I'm sure it's nothing.'

I wrinkled my nose at something distasteful. 'Can you smell that?'

'Yeah.' Josh laughed. 'Pure stink thistle fart. Those bloody flowers.'

'But there aren't any around here, are there?'

Josh looked around. 'Don't think so. Still bloody reeks, though.'

He stood up and yawned theatrically. 'Right. I am going to go and wash this tired face.' He punched me on the arm, gently. 'Get some rest, tiger.'

'Right,' I said. I sat alone on the picnic bench, waiting for Gwen and Anwen to come back.

Eloise

They say we come screaming into the world.

The weird thing about watching a birth is how it's never the same. When I was birthing the Children of Rawbone, I was amazed at how silent it all was. How calm they were, even from the start.

It had been a long night. A night I hadn't wanted to spend alone with my thoughts.

I watched the pod twist and collapse, splitting apart like a time-lapse film of a rotting avocado. Steadily and gently. When I was a girl, I loved spring when the snowdrops and daffodils would poke through the ground, growing so fast you could almost see them moving. Almost. Almost. The times I would spend as a little girl, hunkered down, staring at plants, just seeing if I could detect their movement. I'd even shut my eyes and then open them again, seeing if there was any change. There must be. There absolutely must be. I knew that. I just couldn't measure it. But I knew that that plant was pushing its way up and out of the world, budding and opening.

The same thing was happening here, but now there was all the change you could want. The pod's flesh bubbled and shivered. There was a whispering on the air that went with the steady rattling of rain on the corrugated tin roof. Then the pod split apart with a sigh, the firm green skin of the pod going soft and falling away, releasing a terrible whiff of gas.

Lying there among the rotting leaves was a beautiful young man in a suit. The pod had grown him with a suit. The face was beautiful and calm and tranquil. It was Sebastian. The eyes opened, blinked once and then fixed on me. The eyes were a deep green. They were clear and firm and dancing as he sat up and smiled.

'Hello, Mother,' he said.

I reached out to lift him up.

'No, thanks,' he said. 'I don't need your help.' He stood and shook himself down like a dog climbing out of the sea.

He was so beautiful. I saw that then. You know that awful thing when sometimes you see someone advertising something and they are so beautiful you just sigh? It was very much that feeling. This is what Sebastian would have looked like younger. I guessed it would be another three decades before this version reached his twenties, but he seemed confident, strong, comfortable in his own body. I remembered my own miserable teenage years – the jocks at high school, all high-fives and hell-yeah, and knowing full well my dating pool would always be the Chess League and the Computer Club. Looking back on it now, of course, I realised they were a lot of knuckle-dragging lunkheads, but back then... oh, I wanted one of them to notice me so bad. Funny how monstrous genetics is. If only, if only I could have been happy with my lab partner, dear sweet little Christopher Chung. Instead, as we sat there studying Mandel's experiments with sweet peas, I spent my evenings dreaming about entirely the wrong kind of boy – rather than someone who read books and laughed at my Jackie Mason albums.

Funny how we grow up, isn't it? If only I'd known how things would turn out, then I'd have been happy. If I could just have fancied him a little bit. Poor Christopher. Probably we'd have been married very sensibly now. Couple of kids. All of *CSI* on DVD. Who knows?

Instead, here I was in a freezing shed in the middle of nowhere, very single, very old, and staring at the most beautiful man I'd ever seen. Actually, strike that, I was gawping.

Sebastian caught my look and his smile changed. It was odd, almost sardonic. He didn't say anything, but something in the tilt of his neck suggested that he knew full well. 'The old crone wants me. Good. I can work with that.'

Sebastian stepped forward, bare feet on the cold concrete floor. (So it grew him clothes but not shoes? Odd.) He walked up to me, a firm, confident stride that brought him right up to me. Close. Extremely close. Almost so close that I thought he was going to kiss me. I trembled. I don't know if I was excited or afraid. Instead he sniffed.

'Good morning,' he said. 'Let's get started.'

Then he walked out of the shed.

Gwen

The change came gradually. Or maybe we didn't notice because we didn't leave the caravan for a couple of days. We shut the door and walled ourselves up. Apart from trips out to the laundry hut.

We just held on to Anwen. She was ours again. It wasn't paradise. But it was normality. Horrible, messy, sleep-deprived, grumpy, snappy, smelly normality. Neither of us wanted to change it.

Mrs Harries had been waiting for me as we left the beach. We'd shared a look. A look that was beyond shattered. She'd just looked relieved.

We didn't much care, frankly. We had Anwen back. I didn't care what happened to Jenny now.

Well, I say that. There were times when it felt as much use as being cross with a flatpack wardrobe, and others where I just wanted to go and stand outside her house and scream at her. Rhys talked me down from that. Truth to tell, it was his suggestion that we lie low for a bit.

Mrs Harries came and knocked on the door. We didn't answer. She came and stood at the window. But I was feeding and I just looked at her and shook my head. With a little scrunch that said, 'Sorry, not a good time.'

She nodded: 'Quite understand, sorry to have bothered you.' She walked away into the rain.

Rhys waited a day before pointing out that I wasn't letting Anwen go. Not even to him.

'She's mine,' I said with not even a hint of realising that I sounded crazy.

'Go on, love.' His voice was so gentle and soft it was breaking. 'Get some shut-eye, and I'll change her. Please.'

'OK,' I said. But I didn't hand her over. He took her gently from my arms. I looked up at him and smiled. 'Thanks,' I said.

'Yeah,' he murmured. 'Fighting for a go at a soiled nappy.' He laid her down and went to work, pausing to grimace. 'Green. Funny how you never get used to green poo.'

'Wait till we start her on solid food,' I said. 'It'll get really interesting, then.'

'If we're still changing her when she's 20, we'll have got this one very wrong.'

'Totally,' I said and shut my eyes.

This time the dreams were different. I was back in that bathroom. But I was being dragged forward. Dragged. I was yelling and screaming. I was terrified. I was trembling. The hands that held me were so strong. I fought desperately, I called and I begged.

I could see the white tiles on the walls and the mirror steamed up and the bright light and the cluster of half-finished shampoo bottles.

'I've run you a bath, Mother,' said Billy.

The bath waiting, the taps running.

The hands that held me, dragged me closer and closer to the water.

I struggled and screamed, screamed for Davydd. But no one came.

Then I looked at his face. Billy's face, red and scarred. And smiling at me.

'I'm sorry, I'm so sorry,' I begged him. 'Please don't make me.'

'It's OK, Mummy.' Billy smiled and gestured to the bath. 'The water's lovely and warm. Why don't you get in?'

'Please, don't do this.'

But Billy just repeated the command.

And, sobbing, I obeyed.

I woke up.

It was like one of those falling dreams. Sat in the chair, gasping and floundering. A second's disorientation, like I was waking up in an unfamiliar hotel room, then grasping for Anwen. Realising she wasn't there, panicking. Seeing Rhys standing over me. Holding Anwen. Looking cautious.

'It's OK,' he said. 'She's here.'

I took her from him. Without asking. 'I had the oddest dream,' I started to tell him.

Then realised. Mrs Harries was standing outside the window again.

'We'd better let her in,' I said.

Mrs Harries looked older, like I'd been asleep for ten years.

When I opened the caravan door I already felt worried. She saw my face. But she pressed on with the social niceties.

'Sorry to disturb you,' she said, her hands fidgeting with her coat.

'Come on in.'

'You know, don't you?' Her face was sharp, all tired angles.

I nodded. 'I dreamed again. Was it Sasha?'

'Yes.'

'What?' said Rhys.

'Billy attacked his mother,' said Mrs Harries. 'He filled the bath and made her get in it. We couldn't get to her in time.'

Rhys swore and held my shoulder.

'We could hear... we knew... it's....' Mrs Harries's eyes roamed the room sadly. Then she sat down on the chair, clutching the armrests on it. 'It's the children. I meant to say. They've not been right... not since Jenny... you know...'

'Since she took Anwen.'

'Yes. Your little baby girl.' Mrs Harries shook her head. 'I assumed... we assumed that they felt sheepish, or collective guilt. Or were afraid of us. Of what we might do to them.'

'And what did you do to them?'

Mrs Harries smiled, the tired thin smile of a woman who is mostly steel and sinew. 'I went to the village hall. Most of the parents took their children home. Said it would be fine. I stayed there with mine and whoever else was left. I wanted them all to be safe. In case anything... you know... awful happened.'

'Did it?'

Mrs Harries shrugged. 'I just fell asleep. Sorry.'

'Did you dream?' I asked.

'No dear, I think that's just you. They're no longer interested in my dreams.'

'So what happened next?'

Mrs Harries considered her hands, how tired and wrinkled they were. 'In the morning, they were different... At first I thought it was sheepish.

Guarded. You see, she...' She tailed off.

'Jenny was there, wasn't she?' My voice was sharper than I'd thought it would be.

Rhys made a little *oof*.

Mrs Harries watched the carpet. 'Yes.' Her voice was tiny. 'She was. Mrs Meredith – poor Beth's so ashamed, she didn't want her around any more. Jenny's been ever so odd ever since – almost like she's in a coma. She just kept to herself at the back of the hall and didn't speak. In the morning I noticed she was still sat there. I swear she hadn't moved all night. But the others... they were a little apart from her. As I said, I assumed it was sheepishness. Or shame. But it was something else entirely. Oh my goodness. It was... They were... different. They were colder. They'd withdrawn from her. They were all watching me instead. It was like they were... Oh...' She shrugged helplessly. 'You a dog or a cat person, Gwen?'

'I want a dog,' said Rhys.

'Little Anwen's more than enough of a handful,' I said.

'Yes,' said Mrs Harries, and I think we'd slightly annoyed her. 'It was like they'd gone from wide-eyed puppies to hunting animals. They were sharp. Instead of blank, they were guarded. As though they were all plotting. They frightened me. They were so polite. But it was... sarcastic? Is that the right word? I got scared. When Nerys turned up –' (I noticed Rhys start at her name) – 'When Nerys turned up to look after them for a couple of hours, I came up here yesterday to see how you were. And for a chat. But you...'

'No,' I was firm. 'Not ready then.'

'So I went back. Tried to teach them a lesson. French.'

She talked on, going through the minutiae of the day. 'But it was like they didn't want to learn any more. One of them asked, "Why do we learn lessons, Mrs Harries?" I explained how important it was to learn. To grow. He waved it away. "Yes, that's all very well. But what about you? Do you ever learn lessons?" I said, "Sometimes. Yes. I mean, when we're at school and of course sometimes in later life. But we don't learn like you do." When I said that, he smirked and said, "No, no, you don't."' She shook her head, shuddering. 'I should have understood then. What would happen later. I just didn't think it through. I didn't realise.' She leaned back in the chair, wrapping her arms around her tightly. Like she was knocking the air out of her lungs. 'They laughed then. They never laugh. But they did then. A shared joke.

'The lesson went on pretty much as normal, but it was like I was talking to them and they weren't listening. I'd see a smile break out from time to time – the same smile but on different children. Rippling gently across the room. It was almost as though they were pretending to take notice of me. To care. But it was all a fake. I carried on teaching them. But it was strange. The sentences I wrote out for them. *L'eau est chaud. L'eau est très très chaud. L'eau est trop chaud pour maman.*'

'Oh my god,' said Rhys. I felt a bit sick in my stomach.

'They were planning it, even then,' said Mrs Harries.

Megan Harries

They waited until the sun set. Until it was evening. Then they stood up.

'Thanks for the lesson, Mother,' said Peter, with that little sarcastic smile. 'But it's time to teach you all a lesson of our own.'

They filed out. I cried out to them, told them to think, that if they acted rashly the village wouldn't be the same, that there'd be retaliation... but Peter just turned and looked at me in the doorway, shrugged and said, 'Whatever.'

I didn't know what to do. I thought about running after them but I didn't want... I didn't want them harmed. I didn't know what they were up to.

They told me later what was going on. Billy's dad got home from work. Poor Davydd, pulling up in his tiny, beat-up old car. And there they were. The Scions. Ringing the house. Standing, staring in. Blocking his way.

He tried fighting past them, to get inside. The whole thing was lit up like the fairground by the headlights from his car. Pretty soon people were twitching curtains and coming out of the pub to look.

Davydd had started shouting, and the others were trying too. That's when I turned up. I wanted to reason with them. But they weren't seeing sense. They weren't listening. They were just stood there, holding hands.

Someone threw a punch, but the kid didn't even show that it connected.

'My wife's in there!' Davydd started yelling, over and over.

One of the Scions, my lovely Peter, acknowledged him. 'Your son is in there, too.'

That's when Davydd broke down, howling.

Shortly afterwards the noises came from inside the house. Terrible noises.

None of us could do anything.

I have never felt more helpless.

When the people realised it wasn't going to work, they started arguing with me. Blaming me. Ordering me to do something.

They won't listen to me any more. They won't listen to any one.

That's when I caught the expression on my Peter's face. It was a nasty little smile: 'If only you knew, Mum, if only you knew.' Oh it was horrible.

Of course, someone called an ambulance... but no one came. There's always been a problem with mobiles, but even the landlines are down now. We're cut off. The world is leaving us alone... alone with these children.

They stood there the whole night, you know, circling that little house. Those strange, dreadful flowers grew up around their feet. And the children just stood there, smiling.

Gwen

It was a lot to take in. Worse because I'd seen it all happen.

There was Megan Harries, arms folded, cold mug of tea at her side, staring patiently at me, a little expectant smile on her tired face. As though I was expected to do something. Why did everyone always expect me to do something? I held Anwen closer, tighter, and tried to think. What would old Gwen say at this point?

'And no one called the police?'

'Tony Brown?' Mrs Harries clucked with disdain. 'No bloody good. Never was. Never would be. Years we spent thinking he was just a stupid, fat drunk… but now it's obvious. He's been working for THEM all along.'

'Them?' I said before I thought about it. Whenever someone says 'THEM' you always fear they're about to start talking about foreigners, the EU, or…

'Well, the government, dear.' Oh yes. Or them. 'I mean, someone's had to keep an eye on the village. Make sure we never got much outside help, didn't talk to the wrong people. Made sure the mobile phone companies never got to put up a mast, that the planning proposal for a supermarket was abandoned, that the caravan park got shut down…' She waved her hands around. 'It's odd, isn't it? You assume it would require – I don't know – brainwashing? Guards and things.' She chuckled. 'But you can control a village ever so easily. Make sure a few people are looking the other way, that everyone's pretty much in on the secret, that everyone's got too much to lose... What are we like?'

I squeezed her hand. She squeezed it back. When she spoke again there was a splinter in her voice.

'They were my children. They were good enough... They were good enough for me... What happened to my babies?'

Rhys

I sat there, trying to pay close attention while patting the wind out of Anwen and silently mopping up a tiny puddle of baby vom on my shoulder. Gwen says always to use a bib, and she's right of course, but sometimes it's the tiny acts of rebellion that mean the most, yes?

The two women sat there, hugging. Mrs Harries old and desolate and Gwen charging up, more awake and energised than I'd seen her for months. Almost like she was sucking the life out of the poor old woman.

'Haven't you forgotten something?' I asked.

Gwen shot me a look. Not now, it said clearly. With an undertone of Put The Kettle On. But there are times, bless her, times when she doesn't know best.

'The Secret Underground Base.'

Mrs Harries looked at me. 'The Weather Station?'

I nodded.

'We've just... why, what can Eloise do? We all know she and Tom just sit up there, doing some kind of research on the Scions.'

'Well,' I pressed on, 'if there has been a change – and they're supposed to be looking after the kids – well, don't you think they'd know about it?'

Mrs Harries clucked. 'Oh, poor Eloise. She's

probably rushed off her feet trying to keep up with it all. No wonder Tom didn't come home.'

'What?'

'No dear, poor Josh says there hasn't been a sign of him.'

Gwen stood up, making her own cup of tea a little too loudly. 'Something's wrong up there,' she said, dragging a teaspoon round a mug like it was Quasimodo's bell. 'I'm going to go and investigate.'

'No,' I shouted. I hadn't meant to shout. I lowered my voice a lot. 'I mean... It's wrong. It's dangerous. Please don't. I don't want you going up there. I've only just got us all back together. I don't want to lose you.'

For a second, I thought we were going to have that proper row. That good old proper barney that had been brewing on the horizon like a storm. Instead Gwen smiled. Which was actually more dangerous.

'Who said I was going up there alone?'

We went to the pub.

Yeah. I know. When the going gets tough, the tough go out on the lash. But it's more complicated than that... Actually, it's not. Not at all. Gwen just wanted to find somewhere that contained as many people as possible. Foot soldiers for her crusade. A bloody mad crusade, if you ask me, which is why it would help if her willing volunteers were a bit drunk.

The pub was as grim as ever. But very, very open.

But in order to get to the pub... you had to pass the village green. You had to pass Davydd's house. You had to pass the kids. Standing there, surrounded by a thick field of those dreadful flowers.

They looked like an art installation. If you thought of them like that, it helped. Not as nearly people but as statues that made it somehow manageable. The worst thing was their eyes. They were open, wide open but not looking. You know when someone says of a statue, 'Its eyes follow you around the room'? Well, it was exactly the opposite with the Scions. They weren't watching us. They didn't care.

At the same time it was obvious that they were waiting for instructions. For orders. For something. Maybe just for someone to make the wrong move.

They weren't alone. A couple of their mothers were sat on a bench. Crying. Mrs Meredith had bought along a thermos flask and sandwiches. Megan Harries went over to them.

There was an odd atmosphere inside the pub. Tense, with that odd sweaty tang to the air – it wasn't that the place was open early; it was that it hadn't shut. Everyone had just gone there to drink and mutter and speculate. At first to get in out of the cold, to steady the nerves... and now they were hiding. Someone had even turned on a sports channel that no one was really watching.

I made for the bar. Gwen made for the centre of the room.

'Hey!' she said. Bright smile, police training leaching through. 'Good morning.'

Not much of a reaction. *If we don't look at her, perhaps she'll sit down and shut the hell up.*

The smile got a bit brighter. Bit steelier. 'Where's Davydd?' she asked. A pause. 'Well?'

The sound of a pint glass sliding across a table.

A head looked up. 'Out the back,' rumbled a voice. 'Having a kip.'

'How is he?'

A bit of a snarl, some muttering. A 'How do you think?' But she had their attention. So Gwen seized it. She spoke, a wonderful rallying address. She won them over and she...

Oh, who am I kidding? Sorry. I wasn't listening. You see...

I was stood at the bar sizing up a packet of prawn cocktail when a hand landed on my shoulder.

'Well, look who it isn't,' cooed Nerys.

She was done up to 11.

'Morning,' I said. 'Not gone to work, then?'

She shook her head. 'Not likely. Staying around to see if I can help in any way.' She paused, and her glossy lips spread out. 'Plus the bus never turned up today.' She reached down to Anwen, slumbering in my papoose and waved a bejewelled finger in front of her.

'Are you OK?' I asked.

She snorted. 'You kidding? I'm bloody glad I never had anything to do with those things. Oh my god... you should have seen what they did. They're still out there now, aren't they? It makes it dead creepy whenever you nip out for a fag. I'm asking Paddy if we can just smoke in here.' She shuddered. 'I mean, it'd make sense. And it is an emergency.'

I made a non-committal noise. For some reason there wasn't that much room at the bar. I mean, Nerys was standing ever so close.

'What about you, pet?' she asked. 'You OK? What brings you here?'

'Ah,' I said. 'My wife wants to go see that

191

everything's OK at the Weather Station.'

'Frankenstein's Castle?' Nerys laughed, tossing out her hair and dabbing at the salted innards of a crisps packet with a finger. 'Riiiight.'

'Oh, don't,' I said, feeling awkward and silly. 'What's it like up there?'

'Never been,' she said. 'It's full of science. We all steer clear of it, you know.' She sighed. 'Doesn't interest me at all.' Then she hopped onto a bar stool, her legs swinging against mine. I felt a bit odd, to be frank. She was looking at me and smiling. 'But you do interest me.'

Blimey.

Gwen was still talking. I tried to listen to her, but Nerys was still there. She'd stopped kicking me gently and instead one of her shoes was RUBBING my leg. I looked back at her and she smiled at me. I was suddenly very conscious of the whole thing. No one had ever played footsie with me while I had a baby on my shoulder before. Mind you, people always say you should try new things.

Sudden barman. Guess I'd closed my eyes for a second. 'What are you having, mate?'

Nerys leaned forward. 'Yes, Rhys, what are you having?'

Er. I wondered about a cheeky pint. It was, after all, a bit of an emergency.

'Go on,' cooed Nerys. 'Be a devil.'

Christ, love, I thought, do you ever turn it down a bit?

'Yeah, pint of Druid's Ruin,' I said. 'Have one yourself, Paddy,' I continued, and then faltered – I'd not offered to get Nerys a drink. Best not give the wrong impression, eh? So she leaned forward, cleavage straining against her top. 'I'll have a JD and coke, thanks, love,' she purred.

I watched the beer fill up the pint and something inside me went 'aaah'. Truth. Being chatted up by Nerys – kind of awkward, and a bit odd, really. But the idea of having a drink before noon. Actually, scrub that, the idea of having a drink. You have a baby... well, monks have more of a laugh.

I picked up the pint and turned back to the room. Gwen was still talking, chatting, arguing, making her point, making small talk. It was all very good. She cares. She loves. She's brilliant. She's winning them all over. Then she saw something. And she stopped. Her smile was still in place. Still bright. 'Anyway, I'll leave it all up to you... it's quite important. Back in a moment.'

What had she seen? I thought. Then realised that Nerys was leaning on my shoulder. How had I not noticed that? I took a thoughtful sip of my pint.

Gwen floated towards us across the sticky black carpet like an avenging Boudicca. From nought to in-my-face in under three seconds. Impressive.

'What the hell do you think you're doing?'

It had been quite some time since I'd been caught up in a cat fight. Actually, it'd been ever such a long time since two women fought over me. In fact, it'd really been ages since I'd felt... special. I'm just Rhys. Hold the baby, boil the kettle, there's a love.

'Just having a pint, checking Anwen for wind,' I began.

Nerys slipped smoothly off her bar stool and squared up to Gwen.

Sometimes on a Friday night in the centre of Cardiff you'd see Valley Girls go for it. I'm amazed there wasn't a show about the Battle of St Mary Street on telly. Handbags and hair extensions and zambucca slammers and... and the men all standing back. Nearly ironed white shirts, nervous expressions. We're not stupid. We just know when to hang fire and keep our distance.

Oddly, right then, I was feeling quite nostalgic for Cardiff.

I noticed that Gwen wasn't engaging with Nerys. She was still eyeballing me. 'Oh?'

It turned out, Nerys was not to be ignored. 'No offence, but –' she stepped forward – 'you screaming at him in front of your baby?'

That did it. Gwen reached critical mass. 'And what about you, luv? This is a bloody crisis and you're busy feeling up my husband.'

Interesting moment. A minute earlier, Gwen had been the centre of a charm offensive. Now she was... I dunno. World War Three with good hair?

Nerys shook her head. No, scrap that. She shook her whole self. Not epileptic, more a dog coming out of the sea. She opened her mouth ready to roar, and I caught a blast of her breath. She'd clearly been drinking for hours. 'A crisis, is it? And what do you think you can do about it, eh?'

'A hell of a lot more than hide in here getting lashed,' cried Gwen. 'Those children—'

'Are Mental.' Nerys was using fingernails as punctuation. 'They are Bloody Mental. That's what they are. I always thought so. S'why I'd never have one. You lot, you're all just too damn desperate.' She was now addressing the whole room, and thundering like the PA system at Glasto. 'Take in one of those things? No thanks. You all did, and now you're hiding in here, scared stiff of them. Let's face it. In a few minutes they'll get bored of waiting and they'll come in here to finish us off, you mark my words. So, Supermum, too bloody right I am just gonna get pissed and crack on to the only fit bloke around here. Rhys is well lush, and you treat him like...'

'Steady on,' I said. I'd got the compliment. Shut it down now.

Nerys blinked. But didn't stop. 'Listen, Gwen *bach*, what is it that gives you a right to lecture us all on how to deal with this?'

There was some murmuring at this. Gwen looked startled.

'Listen,' she began, but Nerys wasn't giving her a turn.

'You think you're better than us cos you've popped out a sprog? In the land of the blind, and all that, is it?'

'No!' shouted Gwen. 'No, believe me...' She was suddenly appealing to the entire pub. Her voice cracked. 'Listen to me. Before I came here, I had... considerable experience of this kind of thing. I worked for an organisation. We dealt with stuff like this.'

'Look' retorted Nerys, 'You could be bloody Catwoman, but right now you look knackered and one of your tits is leaking.'

'Oh.' Gwen blushed. She looked down. There was, it is true, the tiniest... listen, occupational hazard with breastfeeding. Frankly, I'm surprised I'm not producing milk by this stage. 'Damn,' cursed Gwen under her breath.

Nerys flung back her head and laughed. Wait, that makes her sound like a Bond villain. And, I suppose, in her own tiny way, in her own corner of a shitty little pub in a forgotten corner of North Wales, she was.

Gwen had shot at alien fleets, she'd faced down forgotten gods, and saved my life. Actually, genuinely saved my life. Rather than just having a spare extra strong mint in a moment of need.

But she had, right now, been beaten by Nerys. A woman who probably knew what a vejazzle was.

Gwen ran out of the pub.

'Sorry, gotta go,' I explained to Nerys. 'It's in the job description.'

Gwen was sat on one of those picnic tables that they set up outside pubs. It was covered in dew and cigarette butts were swimming in an ashtray pond.

'Hey,' I said.

'Don't.'

'I really wasn't...'

'Don't.'

'OK.'

Her hands raked through her hair, grabbed two hunks and twisted them around her fists. 'I just needed you to support me.'

At this point, fellas, please note, there is only one thing to say. It is not 'Well...'

'What?' Gwen stared at me.

'Those kids,' I said, as brave as Indiana Jones tiptoeing across a rope bridge. 'I know you want to go to the Weather Station, but those kids...' I gestured across the scrub of land that had been the village green. It was now covered in those strange plants, their heady scent pungent on the wind. At the other end, swirled in mist, stood about a dozen neatly dressed teenage statues. 'Someone should keep an eye on them. I know... Nerys – well, she's right. They're not going to stand there for ever. I'm going to try and stop them. I've got to.'

'OK.' There are ways of saying OK. It's a danger phrase in a relationship, along with 'fine' and 'I'm just phoning your mum for a chat'. Right now Gwen said 'OK' like she'd run a marathon on broken glass and was about to cook Christmas lunch. She looked so tired and so miserable.

'I'm sorry,' I said. 'I really don't agree with you. I mean, can't we just... you know... divide our forces?'

Gwen held up a hand. Not listening. 'Whatever,' she said, quietly.

We just stood there for a second. I wanted to hug her. I reached out. We looked at each other.

Anwen woke up, loudly.

Gwen took her off me. 'I'll just feed her, then I'll be off. You go back into your pub. Just go, Rhys.'

And she wandered away into the mist.

I went back into the pub.

Eloise

Hiya

   Hope you've had time to take on board our earlier feedback about the Cuts and cycle it into your workflow as rapidly as we'd all like. I'm afraid projects are being lined up and shot down wholesale rather than salami-sliced, and I'm sure you're working your hardest to deliver some clear deliverables ahead of the current direction of travel.

   Small thing. Just wondering how Phase 2 is going downstream at the coalface? I've been checking the shared folder and there's no progress report unless I'm missing it. Thought we'd agreed you'd email something over asap. Guessing you must be too rushed off your feet with stuff, so I'll prioritise getting someone in to work alongside you.

   Looking forward to hearing from you!

   xJasx

Sebastian II smirked. 'Does she always address you like that?'

'Yes,' I said.

'What a bitch,' he laughed.

I blinked. 'Perhaps I should just...' I began, but his hand landed on mine.

'No,' he said, firmly. 'I don't think so.'

'But...'

He arched an eyebrow and his expression was

ironic. Like a Boden catalogue model who knew something you didn't.

'What are you going to tell her, Eloise?'

'Well...'

Tom came in. 'Yes, what are you going to tell her?' Tom looked a mess. His hair had unwound like pencil shavings and there was jam on his shirt. His face looked tired. Jeez, if he looked like that, what must I look like? Probably best not to ask. Mind you, Tom mostly looked furious. 'Go on,' he snapped. 'What are you going to say? Have you seen the reports of what's happened in the village? What they did to Sasha? Your children are out of control.'

Sebastian turned his perfect face on Tom. 'There you are wrong. They are under my control.'

Tom broke, slapping his coffee mug down on the desk. 'You ordered them to... kill...?'

Sebastian nodded. 'She had harmed one of us. So I ordered reprisals.'

'What's happened to you?' Tom yelled. 'You look different...'

Sebastian's hand grabbed Tom's wrist. It wasn't crushing it, or aggressive. Nor was it particularly forceful. But I could tell that Tom was... if not in pain... then at least in quite a lot of discomfort if he moved at all. He froze, trembling slightly.

'The Scions are under new management,' Sebastian said simply. 'I have had a change of mind.'

'Oh my god,' groaned Tom, staring hard at the figure standing over him. So young and so cruel. 'This isn't Sebastian, is it?'

I shook my head, ashamed to admit it. 'No,' I said. 'It's the new version.'

Tom stared at Sebastian with fear. A fear that Sebastian recognised and grinned at. 'Eloise is really very clever. Things have moved on in four decades. The understanding of how to programme the Juniper Tree has improved considerably. I am a much better leader. A stronger soldier. I am much more effective.'

'Right,' sneered Tom. 'And you boiled a woman to death.'

'A fair and just reprisal,' said Sebastian. 'We will not be hurt, not by anyone.' His hand twitched slightly, and Tom fell to the floor, clutching his arm and screaming.

Sometimes you realise when you've made a dreadful mistake and you push it to the back of your head. Probably because you realise what a mess you're now in.

Came the dawn, and I'd put Tom's arm in a sling and pumped him full of painkillers.

'I don't suppose I can go to a hospital, can I?' he asked.

I shook my head. 'Let's not. For the moment.'

'I am in a lot of pain.'

'And goodness me, how Angry Birds must be suffering,' I growled unkindly.

Tom said something quite rude and went outside.

I joined him. You need two hands to light a cigarette. I stole one off him.

I stood there, in the rain, trying not to cough.

He smiled. Uneasy peace. 'We've really screwed up, haven't we, boss?'

'Yeah,' I said. 'Any ideas? What do we do now?'

'Wait?' he asked. 'Sebastian's replacement seems to be very successful.'

'I was rather afraid he would be. Which is why I never activated him before.'

'Plus...'

'Plus I rather loved the old one.'

We stood there silently for a bit longer.

'How do you feel?'

I shrugged, and dragged on the cigarette. 'Running on empty? Is that what you'd say? I want to go to bed and cry for a week. Oh, what have I done?'

Tom groaned. 'It's only going to get worse, isn't it?'

'Yep.'

We stood there for a bit longer. I was aware of how wobbly those damn cigarettes make your legs. I leaned back against the damp brickwork of the Weather Station. I wanted to go home.

That's when we saw her.

Pushing her pram up the path to the fence.

Gwen.

'Hi there!' she called out to us. 'I think you'd better let me in.'

'Can't do that,' I called back.

Gwen grabbed something from a pannier under the pram. It was a set of bolt cutters.

'Sorry,' she said. 'Not a request.'

Tom chuckled. A top secret military base was being broken into by a woman with a pram. 'Nice,' he laughed.

'Yeah,' I replied.

Things were so bad, I figured... well, let her have a go.

The door banged open. Sebastian stood there, his

face set in that empty smile I was learning to fear.

'Morning!' called out Gwen. 'I'm breaking in.'

'No,' said Sebastian. 'Stop. Turn around. Take your baby. Go home. We'll deal with you later.'

Gwen shook her head. 'Not going to happen.' She applied the bolt cutters to the fence and started to snip.

Sebastian's voice carried over the morning rain. 'Mrs Williams, you and your baby... you are powerful symbols to the people of Rawbone. Interesting. I would rather see this preserved for further study.'

'See,' sighed Gwen, snipping away at the fence. 'That's why I've got to break in and stop you.'

'Last chance,' said Sebastian and pulled out a gun.

I felt sick. Sick that he was casually aiming a gun at a woman with a pram. Sicker still because I knew that she wouldn't stop and he wouldn't fail to fire. Sickest because I'd created him.

Gwen looked at him. At the gun. At us. She shrugged and the bolt cutter sank into another link.

Sebastian fired the gun.

One shot.

That was all.

Right into the heart of the pram.

'*The baby!*' I screamed.

Rhys

OK. One of the nice things about having a baby was that for a while our rows had been normal. Lovely bit of nice awkward silence, tread carefully around each other for a bit before making some casual peacemaking comment. You know the drill: 'Would you like me to change her?' 'We're running low on tea.' 'Philip Schofield's not going to get any older, is he?'

Rowing between couples. 'I thought it was your turn to do that.' 'Seriously, would it kill you to put the seat up just once?' 'Shall I put the rubbish out again, then?' Rows like that are what the English language was made to cope with. Nice simple sentence structure. Subject, object, passive aggressive. Strangely comforting.

But now Gwen and I were back to the kind of rows we used to have. Uncharted territory. 'Off out to spend the evening with your handsome immortal alien boss again, is it?' 'Why does hunting down the alien shape-shifter assassin always have to come first?' 'What the hell is that giant fish doing dancing in the living room?'

Here we were again. 'So I let a girl flirt with me while we were surrounded by creepy alien pod children and you're now off to their secret base to try and sort it all out while I'm stuck alone in the pub. Is that it?'

I stood there alone in the rain.

Nerys came out and plonked herself wetly down on the picnic bench. Rain was sputtering down the umbrella. We sat there, glumly staring across the stink thistles at the distant children. Nerys did something slight, rearranging her top. It was freezing, but she showed no sign of feeling the cold.

'It's all right,' she said, placatingly. 'I'll put my claws in.' She shifted over a bit nearer. 'Gwyneth Paltrow gone, then?'

'Yeah. She's going to try and save us all single-handed.'

'Tricky,' said Nerys, chewing gum and pulling at her hair.

'Yeah.'

'You not going after her?'

'Nope.'

'You are always supposed to go after her, if you know what I mean.'

'Yes. I know.'

'And?'

'Sometimes I choose not to.'

'Eh?'

'Sometimes, sometimes, I happen to believe that I am right and my wife is wrong, see?'

Nerys considered this for a bit. 'Brave.'

I smiled just a little. 'Yes.'

Nerys and I sat there watching the kids. They watched us back. Sort of.

She jerked a thumb at them. 'So, what are we going to do about them? We can hardly throw a sheet over them, can we?'

'No,' I replied.

'You'd need a really big sheet for a start.' Nerys

giggled.

'Thing is,' I said, 'they're going to attack us. Sooner or later.'

'You really think so?'

'Let's just say that, in my considerable experience... yes.'

'What?' Nerys looked at me. 'You and Gwen really have experience of this kind of thing?'

I nodded, trying to look modest.

Nerys wasn't fooled. She nudged me in the ribs. 'But mostly Gwen, yeah?'

'Yes,' I admitted. 'Mostly Gwen.'

Nerys

I'm the last child of the village. Born in 1987.

Imagine that, eh? No one to play with growing up, not really. Just me and Davydd and Sasha... and then, gradually... Those Scions. It's not that we ignored them, really. It's just that to start with, they were so much older. You never play with older kids, do you? And they didn't play properly. They tried. But they just liked games with each other. And when you were a little kid, they were creepy, know what I mean? Actually, if you're a grown-up, they're still creepy. Every morning, Sasha, Davydd and me would queue for the school bus. The only children to go to school. The only ones who needed to. And every evening I'd come back to find my mum waiting for me at the bus stop. And she said to me, time and again, 'If ever anyone asks, don't tell them about this place. About the other children here. Cos they'll think you're like them. They'll think you're... funny too.' Then she'd hold me and tell me how lucky she was. To have a normal kid. So I tried so hard to be normal. I guess that's what we all do in life, kind of not stick out. But... you know how it is, growing up in a place that's kind of sad. You feel sad too. You try not to be, but you are. You make it worse.

Being a teenager was hardest. I just wanted someone to tell me that I was doing it right. And no one does. It was just Sasha, Davydd and me –

worrying that, when we got to 15, we'd look and act like the others. Cos the only people you had to compare yourself to was them... I loved it when Mum took me away on holiday. Places like Porthmadog. You know the kind of dive I mean. Like going on holiday in ancient history. The 1970s! Kiss me quick and fruit machines and guys my own age. Well, more or less. My idea of heaven was just to get out of here. To move to a dump like Porthmadog. That's the thing about this place, it sets your sights low. I mean, look at Davydd. Me and Sasha, we were like best friends... until we realised that Davydd was the only chance either of us had. We were teenagers, we were supposed to be fooling around, right, all cheap brandy and bus stops, not looking at the one boy in the village as a potential mate. I remember my mum brushing my hair and saying, 'You got to look nice for Davydd, pet.' Sasha got him, of course. She was so condescending when she won, like Queen Muck, she were: 'Oh Nerys, I hope you're OK now that me and Davydd are going steady.'

I took it, but I knew if I was going to stand a chance of a normal life, I had to get away.

Of course, the joke was on Sasha and Davydd. They were stuck with each other and they got nothing. They tried and tried, and some fancy government doctor came out and treated them – made Sasha ever so sick. But nothing. The day she gave up was the day the village died. And it's never forgiven her for it.

I remember that day, that day when her Scion turned up and Sasha just stood there on the doorstep, sobbing and screaming until Davydd led her back inside. The poor kid waited there for an hour till

Davydd came for it. He'd only gone and made it a bloody cup of tea. Oh, I stood and watched. I stood and I watched and how I laughed. Because it was their lives that were ruined, not mine.

I knew I'd get away – this would be my chance. But I stayed here. Just for a bit. I stayed here for Mum. I remember when I got into my twenties, she asked me if I wanted one of them kids. She said I'd never be able to have one of my own. I'd kind of known that, but I took it hard, all the same. When your mum tells you something, it's got to be the actual truth, hasn't it?

So my only option was to give in, one day, and have one of those kids turn up.

But not yet.

Rhys

Nerys gestured at the patiently waiting crowd of Scions. 'Well, would you want one of them?'

I thought about it. Would I swap loud, messy, demanding, incoherent Anwen for a Scion? Even before they went all Stephen King?

No. Not for a second.

'So what do we do?' asked Nerys gently.

'We run away,' I decided.

Nerys and I left the people in the pub and we went knocking on doors, seeing who was around, who'd open up and talk to us. Bashful and Gobby. We made quite a team. Some people were frightened, others were waiting it out, or pretending there wasn't a problem. We told them all to head to the pub. And to bring along their car keys. That seemed like a good idea. We'd fit everyone we could into cars and go.

'Go where?' asked Nerys.

'Anywhere. Away,' I said.

'Yeah, that's not going to cut any ice with anyone, you know. Stick in the name of a B-road or something.'

I shrugged. 'I think we should just go. We're not leaving for ever. We're just going to a place of safety.'

'Wilkinson's?' Nerys laughed. 'There's one about thirty miles away.'

'Yeah,' I said. 'Let's go shopping.'

By mid afternoon we had everyone together. Well, nearly everyone. Even Josh had come back early from work. Still no sign of Tom. He was worried. We all were. And there was no sign of Gwen. I kept glancing towards the distant Weather Station. Wondering if we'd see a mushroom cloud. But we didn't.

Mrs Harries was the last to turn up. Wrapped up like the French Lieutenant's Woman, laden down with bags. 'Not like we're coming back in a hurry,' she said. Her eyes were so sad. 'Time was when we'd have village outings. Hire a charabanc. Not done that for ages. Ah well. It's time. Let's head back out into the world.'

There was some nodding. Some of the nodding was a bit sluggish, some of the stares a bit glassy. I figured a lot of the people there had been drinking for quite a while. I hoped we'd have enough people sober enough to drive. Hey-ho.

'One thing,' said Mrs Harries. She lifted up a wicker basket. 'For you, dear.'

In the basket was Anwen. Snoring.

Eloise

Gwen fell as Sebastian fired – at first I thought she'd been shot, but it was just a bit of shrapnel from the pram. She lay down there in the mud. Tom and I were already running to her. To her and her baby. We had no idea.

Imagine the relief. The relief of realising that Sebastian hadn't slaughtered the baby.

He locked us up. In the very shed that had given him birth just hours before. The rain was drumming on the tin roof. Thankfully there was the heating lamp in there.

I checked the graze on Gwen's arm and she, Tom and I all looked at each other. I realised the last time I'd seen her, I'd been wide awake and she'd been exhausted. Now our roles were reversed.

'It's at times like this I miss having a gun,' said Gwen. 'Lots of guns.'

'Riiight,' said Tom.

I burst into tears.

Gwen was good about that bit. Really good. Which made me feel worse. She was so kind – she had a sympathetic, naturally interested face. Remember when you were at school and you'd fall over and get a graze on your knee? There was always one teacher with that face. You'd run to that face to dry your eyes, slap on a Band-Aid and give you milk and a cookie.

And yet... there was something about Gwen. Like a candy with a hard centre. That face – it made you tell her too much.

'I killed Sebastian,' I said. 'He was so gentle and kind and wonderful and I killed him.'

'What do you mean?' she said.

I told her what I'd done to Sebastian and she got very angry. Tom didn't look too pleased to hear it again, either. I tried softening my part in it. But I really couldn't make it look good from any angle.

'Poor Sebastian.' I looked up at Gwen, begging her to understand. 'He wouldn't harm a fly. Ever so docile. Not a bad bone in his body. There to greet you every morning. Knew just when you wanted something... but when the other Scions were birthed, they took their mental lead from him. It was like he controlled them. The guiding mind. Which... for the original purposes of the project... Well, there's just no place in the world for nice people.'

Had Sebastian been there, he'd have known what to say. But he wasn't. Because I'd killed him.

'I just couldn't bring myself to do it. His replacement had been ready for years,' I finished lamely, sniffing. 'But I just didn't... I didn't want to do it. But they're talking about closing us down. That's the threat. Government Cuts. Rationalisation. As though any bit of this project was rational. But in the end it all comes down to money.'

'So you activated them?' To give Gwen credit, the smile was still in place. Just about.

'That was the plan,' I told her. 'All along. They'd realised the Scions could make a lovely fighting force. Unswervingly obedient to their leader, following commands without question, able to communicate by thought. But best of all... disposable. Acceptable casualties. Thing is, they let the project slide for a bit... last couple of decades it's just ticked over, really. But then the heat was on. All those losses abroad in all those wars – all those pictures of nice young people who wouldn't be coming home. To you and me, each of those pictures is an unspeakable tragedy... but to your government it was an embarrassment. It was bad PR. War didn't look so good all of a sudden – not when our people were still dying. They've spent a lot of effort on trying to make war look nice and clean from our side – big planes blowing up bases from a distance, while the soldiers build water tanks and fit new roofs on schools with sunglasses and a smile. None of that actual killing. War was starting to look nice and tidy. But not any more. Suddenly it looked messy and horrible and people didn't want any part in it. And someone somewhere remembered the Scion Project. Well, I say remembered – I think stumbled upon it. I think they only really noticed when the woman who founded it... well, she retired. Odd how vast government conspiracies actually work. From the internet you'd assume that it's all run by scary people in giant secret caverns. Actually, this whole project appears to be run by someone in Personnel. She was asked to recruit a replacement to run the project... and so she had to find out what the project was first. And she looked through the file and went 'Jackpot'. She knew she was on to something. The making of her. This tiny little corner of the UK has been paid for and controlled by standing order for years. But she took over and she marshalled it. She turned over a new leaf. She brought me in and demanded I show some results. So I sat down, and I started growing Sebastian II. I'd almost completed it when I realised what a damn stupid thing it was to do. But by that time... I stalled her, but it was only going to work for so long. Poor Sebastian.'

I realised I was crying again, and I wiped away my tears, feeling embarrassed – I'd ended his life. It wasn't really my place to feel sad at his passing, was it?

'He looked at me... ever so trustingly and I still did it. He was beautiful and amazing. I guess as soon as I arrived his days were numbered. I'd do it eventually.'

I noticed how tired I sounded. 'This is the end of the road, Gwen. I've done it now.'

Gwen

So, there I was, locked up in a shed. The wind outside rattled the roof. It was a couple of hours since I'd last fed Anwen, although I'd left Mrs Harries with a couple of bottles.

OK, great example of altered priorities there – that's how having a baby rewrites your mind. I should have been thinking, 'Ah, now, wait, alien super-soldiers on the rampage,' but that's coming in a poor third, some way after 'How many nappies did I leave her with?' Dear Anwen, at some point I would like to get my brain back, please. If Mummy is to try and clear this mess up, then she'd like to be able to out-think a trouser press.

Strangely, Tom took the reins. 'I think we should break out,' he announced, boldly, like he was planning on launching a rocket. 'I am cold, I need painkillers, a hospital, and a slash.'

Funny what motivates boys. Rhys is just the same. I'm all nappies, he's all pot noodle. We are so rocking that cliché.

He grabbed a large pair of scissors off the desk. 'It's something, isn't it, surely?'

Not a lot, as it turned out. I don't know if you've ever tried to jimmy open a padlock from the wrong side of a door with a pair of kitchen scissors, but I can tell you for free that it's a non-starter.

After a few minutes we stood back, Tom sucking

a small cut on his thumb.

'Well,' he sighed, 'that was a bit of a failure.'

'We could always try digging a tunnel,' I suggested.

Eloise didn't laugh. Odd woman. I mean... she'd killed someone. Not even for a reason that she believed in. But because she was scared. And it was like something was loose in her head, and if you shook her brain you'd hear something rattling. Not really the kind of woman you'd want unleashing a murderous alien life form on the planet. On balance.

Eloise stood up, pulling her hands out of her gilet pockets. She snatched the scissors from Tom's hand and marched over to an old sheet of join-the-dots clapboard fastened to one wall, stabbing into it again and again. Tom rolled his eyes. But Eloise was tearing away chunks of the board, revealing an old window.

She stood back, admiring her handiwork. 'There.' She sounded pleased for the first time in hours. 'This was designed to keep people and sunlight out. Not as a prison. Now, I'm too old to go through, Gwen's liable to explode like a milk fountain, so here's the key to the padlock outside, Tom. Go crazy.'

'With my arm in a sling?' he protested.

Eloise nodded. 'Do your best.'

A few minutes later we stood on the darkened runway. What we really needed now was a plan. Stupid Gwen. I'd had all that time to work one out, but I'd got nowhere. It was obvious that Sebastian needed to be stopped. Switch him off and the Scions would be without a leader. But how were we going to do that?

Eloise, though, seemed fired up with excitement, a gleam in her eyes that you could see in the dark. 'We're going to the hangar,' she announced.

We stood in front of the Juniper Tree. Its leaves tangled and rustled. At the base of the tree was a curled-up figure, mostly moss and leaf, but still wearing traces of a suit.

'Oh god,' wailed Tom. 'Sebastian.'

Eloise nodded, but dismissed it. Her brain had hardened like a politician's. She was drawing a line and moving on.

I went over to the body and knelt down as close as I could. The skin was green, but turning rapidly brown, crackling like old paper. There was still an expression of gentle calm on the face. I felt sad looking at it.

Eloise crossed over to a small bench beside the Tree. It was cluttered with equipment that may as well have been labelled 'Science'. Some of it looked like it had been there for over twenty years, but in amongst it all was a shiny new laptop. She stroked it fondly.

'Sebastian, the real one, was always afraid to use this,' she said, with a sad smile. She worried away at some wiring, grinning. 'It communicates with the Juniper Tree, with its creators. Sebastian always said he didn't really need to talk to them to know what their intentions were. I don't know how you'd describe the Juniper Tree best... a space probe, I guess. But this could chat with it directly. It's based on the technology we used to genetically re-engineer the Scions. But it can use the Tree to relay a message. To phone home.'

'How long before they reply?' asked Tom. 'And what the hell would you say to them?'

Eloise flashed all of her wonderful American teeth. 'Ahhh, well, there's only ever been one thing to say,' she said, dusting off a microphone and plugging it in to the laptop. It hummed with a warmth of feedback that caused the Juniper Tree to stir loudly. She tapped the microphone and the Tree rustled.

There was an air of expectation. Then Eloise spoke.

'We have your children.'

Rhys

Convoy! We were on our way, stepping out of the pub. Some people had even got wheelie luggage, the buggers. No one in the history of the world has ever made a stealthy getaway with luggage on wheels. I was carrying a baby in a papoose along with a bag of nappies, and I was a ninja by comparison.

It felt weird leading the charge, but someone had to do it. And it would be me. Well, me and Nerys.

'Come on, yeah?' she said, holding the door open until all the hot air rushed out of the pub. 'Let's get a move on.' She looked magnificent. I'd forgotten how much I missed seeing a Welsh lass in war paint. 'Andalay! Andalay!' she cried, grabbing hold of someone's luggage.

There'd been talk of forming a committee. Of hiring a bus. Of trying to see if we could get through to anyone in authority. The shoddy realisation that PC Tony Brown had already left the village told us all we needed to know. There'd be no help on the way. We were on our own.

It helped that most people were either pissed or in shock. There'd been a small fight between a couple of people over whether or not it had really been that great an idea to pour most of a bottle of vodka down poor Davydd, but he'd stopped projectile vomiting so at least it wasn't so much of a problem getting someone to share a car with him.

I wondered, briefly, if Moses had it like this when they headed out into the Red Sea. 'I mean, yeah, OK, so Pharaoh may be chasing after us, but I was wondering if we shouldn't just do something about food. I know Paddy's got a few pizzas in the freezer out the back. We could warm them up no trouble...'

Give me strength.

What I really mean by that is Give Me Gwen.

Anwen slept cautiously, waking up occasionally to loudly complain at the absence of her mother. I knew just how she felt.

'Can't you shut her up?' snapped someone. 'It's like a siren.'

'This is what real babies are like,' I growled, more angrily than I'd meant. I stopped, feeling a bit guilty. Not the time.

So, we started to weave our way out of the pub.

They waited until we were all on the green before they started advancing towards us.

Thing about a small Welsh village, not much street lighting – just the stars. And the glowing eyes of a dozen alien kids. They started to march across the village green, scything through the flowers. All together. Coming our way.

Someone screamed. Someone fell over.

'Everyone back to the pub!' I yelled. Somewhere inside my head, I found that funny. But it really, really wasn't.

Gwen

'We have your children.'

Even standing in the hangar, the reaction was immense. The rustling of the Juniper Tree became an agitated murmuring. There was a nervous tang in the air. I had the horrible feeling that we had the Tree's full attention, and it was far from happy.

'Listen,' said Eloise, her voice defiant, 'and pass this message on. We have your children. They are under our control. We don't want to harm them. But they may be in danger.' She paused and addressed the tree. 'And tell them about us. Tell them about the humans as a species and about what we are using their children for.'

The leaves rustled and stirred like a storm was coming.

Eloise stood back. 'There,' she said, pleased. 'I wonder what will happen next.'

I felt appallingly worried. I wasn't a trained xenobiologist, but I knew damn well how I'd feel if someone rang me up to say they'd got Anwen and were experimenting on her. My reaction wouldn't be all that rational. I don't believe I'd think it through. And thank god Rhys didn't have any nuclear warheads.

One of the things that happened next was that Sebastian came in. He'd changed out of the suit. Or grown a different one. It was more like an army uniform. His face had changed as well. The neatly combed hair was now shaved to stubble, the placidly handsome face was sharper. And he looked angry. Ever so angry.

If he looked like a military commander, he behaved more like the spoiled kid who finds someone playing with his toys. 'Why did you do that?' he demanded.

Eloise turned around. 'Sebastian,' she said softly, 'I... need to get us help.'

'Why?'

'Because... because I've made a mistake,' Eloise halted, standing up to him with all she could. 'Oh, I am so genuinely sorry. You're not... I'm afraid of you.'

Sebastian took this with a dangerous calm. 'You made me this way, *Mother*. I am supposed to be a military leader. I have my army. My orders are clear.'

'Really?' Eloise looked alarmed. 'I made you, but I didn't give you orders.'

'No,' sneered Sebastian, 'but Jasmine did. Your function ended as soon as you birthed me. Jasmine now deals directly with me. She has issued me with orders and I am fulfilling them.'

'What orders?'

Sebastian paused. For a second his face wore the smugness of a child going 'I've got a secret.' Then his lips thinned. 'The village is finished. I am ordered to rationalise it. To close it down. So I have decided that everyone is going to die.'

Rhys

They started hammering on the door of the pub. We were trying to block it with a fruit machine, but then there were the windows to fasten and the back door to bolt and...

Look, it was a stupid zombie movie situation.

Then it went quiet. That was worse.

All of us, huddled together – the few dozen people of Rawbone, clustered in heaps, waiting. Some were crying quietly. Some were just ashen. Nerys had lit a fag. Josh was helping a semi-comatose Davydd, putting his head between his knees.

Anwen started to wail. People stared at me.

'What?' I said. 'It's not like they don't know we're in here.'

Then I understood why Anwen was crying. It swept across the room – a wave of thought, pressing down on us like a rush of water. The children didn't need to get in. They could just walk into our minds.

Other voices joined in with Anwen's, crying out in fear. Mrs Harries stood up, shaking, shouting that we had to try and think positive thoughts or something – but that was obviously doomed. The negative always wins out.

Paddy and Nerys were screaming at each other at the bar. Paddy was yelling: 'They can't get in, they can't get in!' He was waving a bottle around.

Nerys was bellowing back at him, telling him not

to be so stupid.

Bottles broke and shattered.

Nerys was fighting Paddy for something.

I could see people clutching their heads and falling to the floor.

Nerys was still howling with rage.

I felt my brain pushing out at my eyes. The blood pounding at my head. I was passing out.

Paddy was holding Nerys's lighter.

'They can't get us!' he roared, and sparked up the lighter.

As I sank to the floor flames danced everywhere. I held Anwen to me. Trying to keep my eyes open…

Gwen

'The village will be destroyed,' announced Sebastian.

'You can't!' shouted Tom.

'I'm doing it already. It's so easy. The children have turned on their parents.' Sebastian grinned happily. 'The village was dying anyway. No one's noticed it for so many years. We won't even need a cover story. The post will stop coming, the bus routes will change. And that will be it. No one will come looking for the bodies. And by that time...' He stopped.

'What?' gasped Eloise.

'No,' grinned Sebastian proudly. 'It's a secret.'

No it bloody wasn't. By the time anyone got around to wondering what had happened to Rawbone, it would be far too late. Sebastian and his small army of soldiers were going to start killing and they weren't going to stop, whatever Jasmine ordered.

I think we'd all worked that bit out. Sebastian's firm bearing. His cold eyes. His childish smile. He didn't need to say it. He was having too much fun.

He addressed himself to Eloise. 'So, you've tried telling on me to Mummy?' He smirked. 'The Tree obeys me.'

'No,' said Eloise. 'Your real parents. The creator of the Tree.'

For an instant, Sebastian faltered, then recovered.

Like he had some time left. 'They're so far away. They are so very far away. Why should they care? And even if they do, it'll take them ever so long to get here. No one's coming for you.'

'Sebastian,' I said. 'Do you... do you really enjoy this? Is this what you want?'

'Yes,' he nodded. 'It's glorious. My real parents would be so proud of me.'

He stepped past us, almost as though we didn't matter, and took the controls from Eloise's hand. She handed them over without protest. That was it. She was done.

He held the laptop and smiled carefully. 'I have come here to order more brothers and sisters,' he announced. 'We shall swarm across this land.'

Strange what you fear about aliens. That they're going to land on our world and destroy it. Sometimes that's true. But sometimes, we do terrible things to ourselves.

Sebastian reached forward and worked the computer.

Above us the tree surged into terrible life, the leaves twisting apart, revealing buds. Hundreds of swelling buds.

Rhys

'Stop!'

Well, there we go then. I didn't die after all. That'd be something to tell the baby later. Better get on with the job of living. I opened my eyes.

We'd got out of the pub. Turns out Paddy had done the right thing for the wrong reason. You know how they tell women to cry 'Fire' not 'Rape' when they're being attacked because people always turn and look? It's a basic instinct. We've a primitive fear of flame that overcomes everything. The fire spread quickly, but not half as quickly as we moved.

It was bloody chaos, true enough, but Megan Harries and Josh took charge. Megan grabbed as many people as she could, shoving them towards the back door. Josh pulled Paddy away from the flaming bar. Somehow, we kept it together, despite the panic crowding into our heads. We rushed towards the back door, pouring out – we were running, screaming and yelling, spilling out onto the wet gravel of the pub car park and sinking down.

Of course, in some ways, that was a mistake.

The Scions were waiting for us.

The whole crowd of children stood there, silent and threatening. Ready to kill at any moment. But not. Not yet.

'Stop!' repeated the voice. A girl's voice. No, a woman's voice. Strident, authoritative. In command.

The children stepped aside. Standing there, silhouetted in the flames of the burning pub, was the short figure of a schoolgirl.

'Jenny!' I cried.

I couldn't read her expression. She marched towards me, and I realised the others had gathered around her like a guard of honour. I could hear each tread of her sensible shoes as she approached. Strange how the brain filters sounds. She didn't say anything, I couldn't see if she was smiling. Her head was tilted slightly to one side. Curious. Or appraising. Or…

'Get up, please, Mr Williams,' she said, gently. I noticed again she sounded more mature. She reached down a hand and helped me up. I saw her face for the first time. Lit by the flame, she looked more confident. Gone was the empty-eyed placidity of earlier. Instead, her eyes were clear and focused and the smile was no longer empty. Her round, soft face now looked more angular, and I could have sworn she was wearing make-up. There were flowers in her hair, such beautiful flowers.

'Oh,' I said.

'Hello,' she said.

'Makeover?' I asked.

'Mentally,' she nodded. 'Sorry about earlier, I was working through some stuff. My head is so jumbled. So many thoughts. It's difficult being a grown-up.' She turned to face the village. 'Hello, Everyone! Good evening. I'd just like to reassure you that you're all going to be OK. I realise that might take some believing, but can you have a go for me, yeah? I've got a lot on.'

'Jenny!' cried Mrs Meredith. 'What do you mean? What's happened to you?'

'Hey, Mum!' Jenny beamed. 'It was time for me to grow up. What happened earlier made me realise that something was wrong. I couldn't be a child for ever. And the other children here needed a leader. There is one more of us – up at the Weather Station. He wants us to be angry warriors. I don't agree. I want us to be normal children.' She paused, and her smile was confident, self-aware. 'We won't get that right, but then being a kid isn't about being perfect. We're going to try to be better from now on.'

The other children nodded, all at the same time. Behind them the pub burned away. Not perhaps a great symbol of a new dawn.

'Anyway,' Jenny continued, 'I know that's quite a lot to take in. So we're going to go away now. We must go to the Weather Station. See you later.'

She turned around and strode off, and the children of Rawbone followed.

There was a silence apart from the crackle of burning building.

'OK, then,' laughed Megan Harries. 'Curious comes in all sorts of colours these days.'

'Bugger me,' said Nerys.

Then the heavens opened. And I mean *literally* opened.

Gwen

The sky boiled. Remember that 'It could be you!' lottery advert – kind of like that. The roof of the hangar was torn off. The sky above us seethed with red clouds, glowing and reaching down, pouring light into the hangar. The Juniper Tree stirred and stretched up into the sky which cascaded down around it.

It was, I have to say, bloody impressive.

Sebastian rocked back, hand clamped to his head.

'They're not following me!' he gasped. He spun round and faced Eloise. 'Why not? What's wrong with them? What's happened to them?'

Eloise shrugged. 'I don't know. Perhaps... perhaps you can only push their nature so much. You're a step too far, Sebastian.'

Sebastian shook his head. 'No!'

The Juniper Tree started to shake along with Sebastian, going from a rustle to a roar.

'*No!*'

The voice, when it came, leaked through a loudspeaker. As a voice it was strange, a product of an ancient piece of machinery.

We all stood back.

'*No!*' repeated the voice. '*We have received your message. What has happened here?*'

'Evolution!' cried Sebastian, proudly. 'Humanity

has taken your seed pods and is making them into a mighty army. Even now this seed bank is birthing my brothers in arms. We shall be a mighty force. We shall reach out across the whole planet. We shall give it to you.'

'*We do not want it,*' said the voice.

'What?' Sebastian looked startled.

'*We are explorers. Not soldiers.*'

'I don't understand,' Sebastian cried.

'*Not soldiers.*'

'But… but then why was I created? Haven't I pleased you?'

'*The children were designed to adapt to their surroundings, to learn. What kind of world is this?*'

'A violent one! A gloriously violent one!'

'*Not a world for us.*'

'I can make it a world that you're proud of.'

'*Who did this?*'

In desperation, Sebastian grabbed hold of Eloise. 'She did! She ran the experiments! She created me! She made me!'

The sky shifted and the Juniper Tree reared up. The whole sky was squinting down, glaring balefully at Eloise.

'Oh my god,' she said. 'I was just doing what I was told to… what I was made to do…'

The voice made a thunderous noise. '*You stole our children. You ruined them.*'

Eloise hung her head. 'Yes,' she said, sadly.

'*Why?*'

'Because… because I was asked to.'

'*Why?*'

'It was glorious!' yelled Sebastian, furious at being ignored.

'No,' shouted Eloise. 'I tried not to… but I ran out of excuses.'

'*Excuses?*' The voice rattled the speaker. '*That is not how we do things.*'

'No,' said Eloise, sadly.

'Wait!' cried Sebastian. 'I can make all this right for you!'

'*Will you give us back our children?*'

'Yes!' said Sebastian. 'And I shall give you this world.'

'*Why would you do that?*'

'What other reason could you have?' Sebastian looked puzzled.

'Wait!' called Eloise. 'I can try! I can try and make them good again!'

'NO!' screamed Sebastian. He hit Eloise brutally. She fell back, gasping in shock.

The strange voice gasped. '*What did you do?*'

Sebastian grinned up at the tree. 'It was all her fault. I punished her!'

'*Why?*'

'To make you happy.'

'*Why would this make us happy?*'

'That's all I want you to be!' protested Sebastian.

There was a dreadful pause. '*What kind of world is this?*'

Without thinking, I spoke. 'It's a bloody great one. You're just looking at the wrong bit of it.'

'*Explain.*'

'This isn't what we're about. We're nicer. We're smaller. We're just kind of weird and awkward and all of us trying our best to get through the day. Ordinarily we don't want to kill, or to take what doesn't belong to us, or to do anything nasty.'

'*What are you... about?*'

I pushed a hand through my hair, 'We're about an extra hour's sleep. About another slice of toast, about getting a seat on the bus, about never having enough money, about getting a message from an old friend that makes you drop everything. About having bad ideas but doing them anyway.'

'*But why aren't our children like this?*'

I shook my head. 'They look like us. But they're not.'

Sebastian shoved me aside, screaming at the Tree. 'Don't listen to her. We are better than them! Her evidence is selective!'

'Of course it is!' I shot back. 'This is just my point of view. It's not evidence. I'm not arguing for my species.' Well, maybe I was. 'We do terrible things to other people and to each other for the stupidest of reasons. We have such short lives and we waste them. We are dreadful. I can't think why anyone would want to be like us.'

'*But we do. That is how we learn.*'

'And what have you learned?' I asked it.

The vines twisted, awkwardly. '*It has been a good way. Previously.*'

'My way is better,' snarled Sebastian. 'Look at me! They stole your children, perverted their creation... but have made something magnificent.' He pounded his chest, proudly. 'I am a wonderful accident. Your children are the true owners of this planet. Not these...' He indicated me, Eloise and Tom with a wave that said 'these old things'. 'Me. I am the child of the future. I offer you this world.' And he smiled.

The Tree fell silent.

Eloise stood up, warily and joined me. 'Imagine

that,' she said. 'All those other planets welcoming these seed pods. A race of kindly, noble explorers. And we spend so much time imagining invaders... that we turned their children into them.'

'It's so human of you, Mummy,' taunted Sebastian.

Eloise stepped forward and stared up at the plant. 'I am so sorry. It's all my fault.'

The Tree stirred again.

'*You accept responsibility?*'

Eloise nodded, ever so quiet and sad. 'Just... just enough of it.' She made a gesture, her hands helpless. 'My parents taught me to own up before you got found out.' A tiny, sad little smile. 'My brother and I used it against each other, terribly.' She paused. 'But it was a system of sorts. It worked for us as a family. So...' She patted Sebastian on the shoulder. He turned away from her. 'I'm saying now. I'm sorry, Sebastian, for what I did to you.' She looked up at the Tree. 'And I am sorry for what we have done to your children. There is much you could have learned from us. Instead you've just learned to fear us. And I can't say I blame you.'

There was another pause.

'Are you finished?' asked Sebastian.

Eloise nodded.

Sebastian broke her neck.

'There!' he beamed.

Rhys

We all stared up at the sky. Anwen started to howl again. She clearly had her mother's instinct for knowing when the world was going to end.

'It's all right,' I said, lifting her up to my eyes. 'Daddy's here. Daddy's going to make it all OK.' Daddy was lying through his teeth.

I had hoped we'd escaped all of this. We'd left Cardiff, our old friends, our whole life behind us.

We'd started again. Because of Anwen.

But suddenly it was business as usual. Strange lights in the sky, and Gwen elsewhere. Trying her best to sort it all out. I had thought that, if ever something like this happened again, at least we'd all be together. Instead, no such luck.

Which left me with very little to do, other than to look after Anwen as best as I could, while the sky above us glowed blood red.

Josh and Megan Harries were standing next to me. 'Never seen anything like this before,' announced Josh. He had the forced casualness of someone who was determined to talk about the weather, no matter what else was happening.

Megan clearly didn't think much of this as a line of conversation. She was pacing around nervously, and then began to play with Anwen, an element of nervousness in her cooing and finger-waving. As though, if Anwen smiled, then maybe it would all be all right.

I looked around us. At Nerys, with soot in her hair, at Davydd, slumped despairingly on the gravel of the pub car park. At the rest, looking up into the sky. No one was telling us anything. There was nothing to go on. No one was even going to lie to us and say there was nothing to worry about.

I just hoped that whatever happened would be quick.

Gwen

Eloise's neck broke with a wet snap.

There was time for three different expressions on her face – surprise, fear and pain. Then she fell to the floor with a sigh, her empty brown eyes staring up at the Tree.

'Bones and water,' announced Sebastian to the Tree. 'That's all they are.'

Tom was making a noise, so Sebastian hit him. I stayed quiet, sizing up what to do.

'One down,' Sebastian shrugged, then implored the tree. 'Now, more. Give me my brothers.'

The tree shook and rustled, the leaves peeling back and the pods swelling. They started to droop to the floor.

Sebastian rushed to the first one. The pod split and ruptured, shrivelling to a husk as a copy of himself forced its way out.

The newborn Scion stood up and opened its eyes. They were clear and blue and they stared around at the world in momentary wonder, taking it all in. He reminded me of Anwen when she first wakes up of a morning. Surprise, wonder, working things out in equal measure. Then the Scion's face changed. It knew why it was here. It smiled, but it was a smile of triumph. He and Sebastian grasped each other warmly.

'Welcome,' said the older Sebastian. 'There is no

time to waste.'

Around them other pods split and cracked and dozens of other Scions began to fight their way out. It was beginning. The air filled with the terrible stench of those flowers.

This was Sebastian's moment, and the triumph flowed across his face. The new Scion's features moulded themselves into a mirror of Sebastian's, and, for an instant, the two wore identical expressions. Then the new Scion frowned, puzzled.

'What?' demanded Sebastian, but the new Scion didn't answer him. Instead his eyes passed over the room, confused. His mouth opened, and a series of clicks emerged. A hand reached up to his head, holding it like it hurt, and then he broke away from Sebastian, staggering backwards, reeling.

'What is happening? What?' cried Sebastian, reaching out for his brother. The Scion fell back, withering and collapsing into his shell with an agonised hiss.

Around Sebastian, the other new Scions were flailing unsteadily. Some had not even managed to leave their pods, and a steady hammering came from inside them as the half-emerged figures started to writhe.

Sebastian, surrounded by dying copies of himself, screamed. 'What's wrong?'

The Tree shook. '*You.*'

'What?' He glared up at the twisting branches. 'What do you mean?'

The leaves rubbed against each other, rustling and crisping.

'*You... sicken us. Your thoughts are poison.*'

A giant leaf drifted to the ground by Sebastian.

The edges were brown, autumn spreading to the heart of the leaf within seconds.

'What?' Sebastian cried.

More leaves started to drift to the ground, crumbling as they went.

'*We will have nothing more to do with you. You are not our child.*'

It was the last thing the Tree said.

Sebastian stood there screaming, but the only sound from the speaker was a rising whine of feedback which ended in a crackle..

More leaves fell around Sebastian, along with rain, pouring through the roof, pelting the tree, shaking the branches bare. The floor of the hangar turned to a mulch of decomposing leaves and worse, a brackish sludge that covered Eloise's body.

Still the leaves tumbled slowly down, and still Sebastian shouted at the barren Tree.

Tom and I held on to each other. There was nowhere to run, no shelter, just this endless downpour.

Eventually, Sebastian stopped shouting. The skeleton of the Juniper Tree stood over him, the air thick with the smell of decaying leaves.

Sebastian turned around, and faced us. He did not look defeated, or sad. He just looked angry.

'You.' His voice was hoarse from the shouting, and rain poured down his face like tears. 'This is your fault. This is all your fault.'

'No,' I told him. 'This is all you.'

Sebastian strode towards me, his face twisted with unthinking, childish rage. Just like Jenny, he was suddenly so very, very human.

Sebastian's walk broke into a run, his arms balling up into fists. I didn't really see him coming.

Or perhaps I didn't know what to do. I was just tired and wet and cold and he was bearing down on me like a lorry.

Tom stood in between us. 'No!' he shouted, but Sebastian struck him aside, and he went down, vanishing in the dead leaves.

Then Sebastian was there, grasping hold of my shoulders, hissing with rage and fury, pushing me down to the ground, his hands sinking into my neck.

It was all happening so fast. Old Gwen Cooper would have done something more than this, at least have fought back. But I was just lying there as he strangled the life out of me. Funny that. The last thing I'd ever do was to let myself down.

The hangar doors swung open. I heard the noise over the pounding of blood in my ears.

Figures walked in. I saw their feet as they crunched through the slush of fallen leaves.

The Children of Rawbone had come home.

Sebastian noticed them, panting with exertion. His grip on my neck slackened and he stood up, facing them. The smile sprang back to his face.

'Your father welcomes you,' he said.

Rhys

Tense moment.

You know there are some people who are just out-and-out shits? Life's Teflon-coated weasels. It's never their fault, they did nothing wrong, every breath is a chance to make themselves better and you worse. They're in every school, every football team, every office. And they're always getting another chance.

The most important thing in that hangar was Gwen. Sitting in the mud. Alive and well. I ran to her, helping her up.

She grabbed Anwen from me and laid her across her shoulder, delighted.

'What are you doing here?' she mouthed.

I smiled. 'Finding out what happens next.'

A neat young man stood over us, his handsome face made ugly by the emotions on his face. You could tell he was a nasty bit of work and he was bloody delighted to see the Scions.

The children of Rawbone walked silently towards him. So was this what had been controlling them?

'Come to Father,' he beckoned. 'I have work for you.'

And they came, kicking up the leaves like it was autumn. He stretched out his arms to them like he was preaching to Saturday shoppers outside Topman. The children stood, heads bowed, unaffected by the rain still pouring in around them.

'Good.' The man smiled. As well as the triumph, there was a definite note in his voice. A sound that said, 'I am getting away with it.' I decided then and there that this wasn't really the kind of bloke that I'd have much truck with.

Which was, of course, when Jenny stepped out of the crowd.

'No, Sebastian,' she said. There was something in her tone. Disappointment.

He glared at her.

'No,' she repeated.

'You are all my children!' Sebastian repeated.

Jenny shrugged. And all the children of Rawbone shrugged too.

'You don't deserve to be our father,' she said. 'You've made us do bad things. You've destroyed the source of our life.' Sebastian was shaking his head at her, desperate, but she carried on talking. 'You're not up to the job. You're rubbish.'

'What?'

Jenny grinned, a natural, unaffected grin. 'We don't need you any more.'

The rain stopped and the sky above us started to clear, blue forcing its way through the strange clouds. A little bit of sunlight fell on Jenny, as saintly as a Disney Princess. All she was lacking was a bluebird landing on her shoulder.

Jenny didn't break eye contact with Sebastian. She carried on speaking. No longer to everyone in the room, just to him. 'We're alone now. They've gone. It's time to grow up.'

Her grin broadened, becoming more encouraging. 'It's OK, Sebastian. It's over. Come here.'

Personally, I'd have happily watched him bugger

off, but I guess that's family for you.

Sebastian took it calmly. He walked slowly through the sludge, his head held down, compliant. He reached Jenny and stood before her, motionless.

Jenny reached out as though she was going to hug him, but stopped. Sebastian didn't respond. Didn't move.

Finally he spoke, his voice a whisper. 'It is never over.'

He looked up at Jenny then, his eyes narrow with fury. He was literally shaking with rage. A hand flew up to strike her... but then it froze.

Sebastian, Jenny, everyone in the room was staring at that hand. It was withered, an old scarecrow's twig fingers. The sleeves of his coat fell away, the fabric drifting to the ground, exposing a stick-like arm. Repelled, Sebastian flexed and stretched the arm, the fingers of the hands snapping and crumbling, the joints turned to powder. He twisted to face the giant tree above him, and as he did so, one of his legs gave way under him, with a snap. As he fell, his head flew back, vanishing into the wet leaves with a dry rasping shout: 'No.'

'Sleep now, brother,' said Jenny, very quietly. Her voice was no longer empty of expression. There was a gentle sadness to it.

She patted her palms together, as though removing invisible dust from them.

She stretched out her hands, and the other children formed a ring, all standing there, staring up at the strangely sad sight of that giant dead tree.

Later, she'd stand on the village green, the other children behind her. As the sun rose, those strange plants finally opened their buds up, spreading out the most beautiful flowers, in every colour, and releasing a rich, sweet scent.

'We are orphans now,' Jenny said to the whole village. 'That is…' And she paused and looked up at the people of Rawbone. Then she smiled that winning little smile. 'If you really want us to be.'

Gwen

That was kind of it, really.

We'd spent so much time projecting onto those creepy kids we'd made them what we wanted them to be. Somehow wrong. Somehow bad. But they weren't. They were blank slates.

Life got back to normal. Megan Harries started her school up again. Nerys helped out pretty much full time. I'd like to say Rhys and I finally got a decent night's sleep, but miracles don't happen. People just got on with their lives. For some of them, it had been a very long time coming.

I'm not saying it was easy. People don't forget being terrorised easily, even if it was of their own making. Davydd moved away. He wasn't the only one. A few people just slipped off into the night. They were helped by a sudden and large amount of money.

Tom arranged that bit of it.

Tom

Hey Jasmine!

Can I run something past you quickly? Small thing, but the Rawbone Project is over. Eloise is dead. Sebastian is dead. The Juniper Tree is dead. The children are all growing up. They've got a new leader. One who isn't interested in being a soldier, but in being a normal teenager. Already they're looking a bit older, dressing differently. The other day, I caught one trying to drink cider in the rain behind the bus shelter.

What I'm trying to say is that Rawbone has children again. Your experiment has failed.

The other thing you should know is that we have all your emails. Sebastian – the real, proper Sebastian – printed them all out and filed them. Along with every other piece of paperwork associated with the project. We've used the photocopier in the village shop (five pence a sheet, receipt attached) and we made lots of copies. One for each family and child. I think that, if you ask very nicely, you can come to some kind of arrangement. They're not greedy people – but you've done a dreadful thing to them.

That's the other thing. Sebastian found the records on those old computers of how it was done. And dutifully printed it all out. How the villagers were denied children. That was the real start of the dreadful experiment in Rawbone – over thirty years ago, a piece of alien technology was tested here, to see if it really would sterilise an entire village. A very (well-documented) success. God alone knows what you've used it for since, but you left quite a mess behind. It's not all bad news, you'll be thrilled to hear. Jenny Meredith (that's their leader) has looked at it all. She reckons there's a way to overcome it. To give Rawbone real children. But she says it's going to be costly. Luckily, we've got you to call on, and we know you'll give this project your full support.

Like I said, the people of Rawbone aren't greedy. They just want what's due to them.

Don't, by the way, think of sending anyone in. Some people are moving on from here. And they've got all the information they need to bury you.

Anyway, I hope all that makes sense and I'd really appreciate you having a look at this if you've a moment to spare. Bank details are on the shared server. Let me know if you have any problems.

Look forward to a quick reply,

xTomx

Rhys

Pity really. The potatoes I'd planted were just starting to come up. I'd be sorry to leave them behind, but there we go. You can't have everything. The day the phone lines started working again in Rawbone was the day Gwen started packing.

I walked down into the village, to say a quick goodbye to a few people. We knew it wouldn't be long.

Tom and Josh were in, their little cottage full of clutter and half-read newspapers. Tom leapt up. 'Sorry about the mess,' he said, his hair a carroty mess. He even had a small thatch of red stubble. 'It all goes to pot when you've not got work on. Billy keeps on offering to tidy up, but I've told him there'll be none of that.'

Billy came in, polite and neat. He'd made an effort to wear a hoodie and some jeans, but even the jeans looked ironed. 'Would you care for some tea, Mr Williams?'

Tom rolled his eyes. 'Josh!' he called, fiddling with his phone.

Josh came barrelling down the stairs. 'What now?'

'Talk to the child.'

Josh sighed theatrically. 'OK then, young man. For a start it's "Kettle's on if you want anything." And for another thing, you are 15. You don't offer to do anything for anyone. I caught you doing the washing-up again this morning. Never again.'

'Sure,' said Billy. He leaned over Tom and pointed to his phone. 'Surely you can get both pigs with the Boomerang bird if you do this...' He tapped the screen, and Tom's face fell.

'Damn,' he groaned.

'I am sorry,' said Billy.

'Another thing!' scolded Josh, resting an arm on Tom's shoulder. 'No apologising. Just assume everything is our fault. It always will be for about the next ten years.'

'OK,' said Billy. He didn't look at ease with it, but he was trying.

Tom didn't look up from his phone. 'No, say it again, but with muttering.'

'OK,' muttered Billy. He went to the kitchen and made us tea anyway.

Josh flopped down on the sofa next to Tom, who gestured to a chair covered with the weekend's papers. I nestled among the travel pages.

'So...' I said. 'If I'd known I'd have bought a card from the village shop.'

Josh and Tom looked at each other. It was a look that said they'd made the decision, but they weren't exactly comfortable with it.

'Look,' began Tom, and then stopped.

'We had to,' finished Josh. 'I mean... no one offered to take him in.'

'When Davydd left... after what happened... well, no one else wanted him.' Tom stopped. Awkward. 'I felt responsible.'

Josh tutted. 'It's a relief, I suppose. And rather modern.'

'Shaddup,' growled Tom. 'Turns out having a kid is rather fun.'

Josh poked him idly in the ribs. 'We may actually make good parents.'

'Plus he empties the cat's litter tray.' Tom looked delighted. 'And it allows me to think that I'm not just slobbing around... I'm setting him an important example.'

Billy came in. 'We're out of milk,' he announced curtly, and poured a cup for himself. 'OK if I go upstairs?'

'That's my boy,' laughed Tom. 'They grow up so fast.' He called out to Billy, 'Have another scrub of your face – I swear you're getting spots.'

'Am I?' asked Billy. 'Would that be normal?'

'Bloody normal,' said Josh. 'It means you're becoming a man.'

'I see,' said Billy, and went upstairs.

'So,' asked Josh, considering me carefully. 'Where are you off to next?'

'I have no idea,' I said, truthfully. 'But we are going. Sharpish.'

'Really?'

'Yes. I think... I don't think we're needed here any more.'

Gwen was waiting for me impatiently, the car stuffed fuller than a Christmas hamper.

Jenny Meredith had helped her pack, the two of them keeping a slightly awkward truce. Jenny stood back. 'Thank you,' she said.

'That's OK,' said Gwen, and smiled at her. 'You'll be fine.'

'I hope so,' shrugged Jenny. 'But we'll see.' She

nodded to Anwen. 'Goodbye.' Jenny turned on her heel and skipped away.

Gwen and I watched her go.

'Right then,' Gwen exhaled, like she'd been holding her breath. 'You're reading the map and I'm driving.'

I waved at Anwen on the back seat. For a moment she considered waving back, then her eyes drifted closed.

Gwen jumped into the car and revved the engine. I sat down next to her with a pile of Ordnance Survey maps. No Satnav for us. We were running away old school.

'How long do you think we've got?' I asked.

Gwen stared up into the sky. 'Well, no sign of any helicopters.' She smiled. 'Maybe that means we're less important.'

In the distance, I could hear traffic approaching from the nearby hills. It could just be a local bus and a couple of cars. Or it could be something else. Time we were off.

'Best not risk it,' I said.

'Yeah,' agreed Gwen. She sneaked a look back to check Anwen was strapped in, and then we drove off.

We sped through the village, past the rows of quiet little houses, the streets full of those beautiful flowers. As we left it, Rawbone seemed different. For one thing, I could hear the sounds of children playing.

Acknowledgements

Thanks to Helen, Lucy, Jac, Jess, Gemma, Beth and Gary for baby-rearing info. To Russell T Davies for advice about breastfeeding. And to the Affection Unit for a variety of remarkable hats.

Available now from BBC Books:

T O R C H W O O D
Long Time Dead
Sarah Pinborough

£6.99 ISBN 978 1 849 90284 7

Cardiff Bay. The government has ordered the
excavation of the wreckage of a secret underground
base. DCI Tom Cutler is watching from a distance,
fascinated by the process. There are people in his
dreams. People he feels he should know.
The disbanded Torchwood Institute spent a century
accumulating non-terrestrial artefacts and catching
aliens. Who knows what – or who – might still be intact
down there.
But by the time they find the first body, Suzie Costello
is long gone…

Based on the hit series created by Russell T Davies,
Long Time Dead is a prequel to *Torchwood: Miracle
Day*, starring John Barrowman and Eve Myles as Jack
Harkness and Gwen Cooper. It features Suzie Costello,
as played by Indira Varma, and Andy Davidson, as
played by Tom Price.

Sarah Pinborough is an award-winning writer of novels
and short stories, including *Torchwood: Into the Silence*
and 'Kaleidoscope' in *Torchwood: Consequences*, and
was a frequent contributor to *Torchwood* magazine. Her
latest novel is *The Shadow of the Soul*, the second book
in the trilogy *The Dog-Faced Gods*.

Available now from BBC Books:

TORCHWOOD
First Born
James Goss

£6.99 ISBN 978 1 849 90283 0

Gwen and Rhys are in hiding. But the isolated village of Rawbone is no place to bring up a baby. With the locals taking an unhealthy interest in their daughter, Gwen and Rhys start to realise that something is very wrong in Rawbone – something with echoes of a life they thought they'd left behind.

As they uncover the village's terrible past, Gwen discovers that Torchwood will never leave her behind – but now she and Rhys stand alone in defence of the Earth. And the children of Rawbone can only bring her closer to the secret forces that want her out of the way.

Based on the hit series created by Russell T Davies, *First Born* is a prequel to *Torchwood: Miracle Day*, starring John Barrowman and Eve Myles as Jack Harkness and Gwen Cooper, with Kai Owen as Rhys Williams.

James Goss is the author of two *Torchwood* dramas broadcast by BBC Radio 4 and co-writer of the official website for *Torchwood* Series One. He wrote *Almost Perfect* and *Risk Assessment* for BBC Books' *Torchwood* series, and the Torchwood audio originals *Department X* and *Ghost Train*, and was a regular contributor to *Torchwood* magazine. He also wrote *Being Human: Bad Blood*, *Doctor Who: Dead of Winter*, and the award-winning audio original *Doctor Who: Dead Air*.